SUNSET CITY

Melissa Ginsburg was born and raised in Houston and attended the Iowa Writers' Workshop. She is the author of the poetry collection *Dear Weather Ghost* and two poetry chapbooks, *Arbor* and *Double Blind*. She teaches creative writing and literature at the University of Mississippi. *Sunset City* is her first novel.

SUNSET CITY

MELISSA GINSBURG

FABER & FABER

First published in 2016
by Faber & Faber Ltd
Bloomsbury House
74–77 Great Russell Street
London WC1B 3DA

First published in the United States in 2016
by HarperCollins Publishers
195 Broadway, New York, NY 10007

Printed and bound by CPI Group (UK) Ltd, Croydon CR0 4YY
Designed by Suet Yee Chong

A CIP record for this book
is available from the British Library

ISBN 978–0–571–32670–9

FSC
www.fsc.org
MIX
Paper from
responsible sources
FSC® C101712

2 4 6 8 10 9 7 5 3 1

to Chris

Where are the arrows that have bandages
Instead of feathers at their ends

SUNSET CITY

CHAPTER ONE

It had rained hard through the night and now the water raced and swirled, overflowing the ditch in front of my building. Houston was always flooding, the whole city built atop paved wetlands. The storm kept the sky dark, and the streetlights glowed through the morning. I stepped into my rubber boots and splashed to the barbecue shack around the corner. I ordered a baked potato filled with butter and sour cream and bacon and slow-smoked brisket, then bought beer at the liquor store next door. On the walk home, the temperature began to rise and moisture thickened the air.

As I approached my building I noticed a guy on my landing. I didn't recognize him. I figured he must have the wrong apartment.

"Who are you looking for?" I called to him.

"Charlotte Ford," the man said.

He stood under the awning above my door, a curtain of rain enclosing him on three sides. He had rough, dark features: hooded eyes, strong jaw, and a blunt Irish nose that softened his appearance. I liked how he said my name.

"That's me," I said. "Have we met?"

"No."

He stood aside to let me out of the downpour. We crowded into the space, walls of water around us, while I dug for my keys. Rain fell from his hair onto his nose and he wiped it away. I smiled without meaning to, because he was so handsome and close. I got the door open and backed into the apartment, set my food on the front table.

"Detective Ash," he said. "HPD."

In an instant I thought of every law I ever broke, trying to figure out how much trouble I was in. Cops always scared the shit out of me—a reflex from the old days, from when I was dealing.

"You're Charlotte Ford?" he said.

I nodded.

"Could I come in?" he said.

"Okay," I said, pretending to be calm.

He stepped inside and glanced around. We were both dripping water on the floor. I took my shopping bags into the kitchen, stashed the beer and the food in the fridge. The detective followed and leaned against the wall, watching me. He took up too much space in the room. I felt claustrophobic, trapped. I was sweating in my raincoat, bright red rubber, its canvas lining dotted with unicorns.

"You know Danielle Reeves?" he said.

"Yeah, I know Danielle."

I should have figured it had to do with her. Danielle was my oldest friend, the only person in the world who understood where I'd come from. I'd hardly seen her in the last few years, but that didn't matter. I was ready to bail her out, lie, provide an alibi—whatever she might need. She was my friend. I would protect her.

"What's this about?" I said.

"I'm afraid I have some bad news," he said. "Danielle Reeves is dead."

"What?" I said.

"Danielle is dead," the detective repeated.

"Dead?"

"She was murdered," he said, watching me carefully. "Let's sit down."

We went to the living room and I sat on the couch. He took the chair by the window. A watery spill of streetlight outlined his face.

"Are you sure?" I said.

"Yes."

"That's crazy. I just spoke to her."

"When was that?"

"Two days ago. Sunday evening. We met for a drink."

"And yesterday?" he said.

"Yesterday, no, I didn't see her. I haven't talked to her since Sunday."

"Where were you last night?"

"Here. It was raining. I didn't go out."

"Can anybody confirm that?"

I shook my head. He wrote in a notebook. I became aware of the shattering rain on the cars outside. I felt for a cigarette in the pocket of my raincoat. Water dripped from it and soaked the upholstery. I always took off my raincoat and hung it on the hook by the door. Why hadn't that happened? My mind rushed, confused, like the current in the gutter—I couldn't get hold of a thought.

I lit the cigarette, took a drag. The smoke hovered around my head, weighed down by humidity.

Ash said, "Danielle's mother tells me you and Danielle are old friends."

I tried to speak but my throat constricted, and I began sobbing. I observed myself, curious and dismayed. I didn't even understand the situation, yet here I was crying in front of a stranger. None of it made sense. My cigarette fell from my hands. The detective picked it up and stubbed it in the ashtray on the windowsill. A part of my brain thought of how I must look: no makeup, snot, the terrible sounds coming from my throat. I grew more and more embarrassed, which made it harder to compose myself. It took a while before I could breathe normally.

The detective stared at me like you would a sculpture, without caring what it thought. What he was saying about Danielle, it couldn't be real. It didn't make sense. She had already survived all the drugs and prison. She was finally doing okay.

"She can't be dead," I said.

"She is, Ms. Ford."

"Not murdered. It's ridiculous. If she was going to die it would've happened before."

"What do you mean?" the detective said.

"Forget it," I said.

He wrote in his notebook again and spoke. "Tell me about the night you saw Danielle."

"We met for a drink."

"Was that a regular thing?"

"Not exactly," I said. "We sort of lost touch."

"When?"

I looked away, said nothing. It was a few years back, in the middle of the drugs and her arrest, but I was not about to talk about that with this guy.

"When she went to prison?" he asked.

I hated that he knew that about her. I saw her from his

perspective—a stripper, a drug addict, a felon. I could see the judgment in his eyes, the dismissal.

"You don't understand," I said.

"What do I not understand?" he said.

"She's not a junkie or some stripper whore. That's bullshit."

"Ms. Ford, take it easy. I'm trying—"

"Leave her alone. You can't assume, because she went to prison—you don't know anything about her!"

I hadn't meant to stand up, or to talk so loud. The muscles in my legs tensed and trembled. I wanted to kick something, to run and run.

"Okay," the detective said. He stood, too. He didn't look friendly anymore. "Come with me," he said.

"Where? Why?"

"To the station."

"Are you arresting me?"

"Not unless I have to."

He took my arm and pushed me to the door, waited while I closed and locked it. We went to his car, a green SUV parked in the middle of the street, alongside the deep gutter. I stepped in a puddle and water leaked into my boots. He opened the passenger-side door and stood there until I got in. He silently steered to a strip mall on Richmond and parked in a lot full of cop cars. Inside he guided me past a cluster of uniformed guys and a roomful of desks. Benches lined one wall. A black kid, about fifteen years old, sat at one end, wrists cuffed, looking at the floor, at his untied shoes. Loud and ugly, the place banged against my eyes. The detective showed me into a dank windowless room with a table and a chair and a camera mounted inside a steel cage. The lights buzzed from the ceiling.

"Wait here," he said.

He left, closing the door behind him. The molded plastic chair was missing one of the bolts that attached it to the metal legs, and it rocked and bent as I shifted my weight. The walls were green concrete blocks, interrupted only by the door and a dark mirror across from it. I glanced at my reflection once—my face pale and bedraggled, strands of wet hair stuck to my cheek—and didn't look again. I kept thinking, I shouldn't be here. There's been a mistake. I got out my phone and tried to call Michael, my boyfriend. I wished I were with him in his cozy apartment, or back at home, or anywhere else, really. But it was no good, I couldn't get any cell reception.

A crack in the cement floor showed where the foundation had shifted. Damp seeped in and I remembered the rain outside. The ceiling lights hummed, muting the distant voices and ringing phones. No way could Danielle be dead. She was the most alive person I knew.

The detective came in with a chair and a manila file folder.

"I'm not interested in judging your friend. I'm not making any assumptions about her," he said. "You're wrong about that."

He opened his folder and slid some photographs across the table. One fell on the floor and I bent to pick it up. He watched me, his arms crossed, his foot tapping the floor.

"Nobody," he said, "no matter who they were, what they did, should go through this. It was terrible, what happened to Danielle. I am trying to find out who killed her. I'm not judging her. I'm looking for information."

I examined the picture in my hand. Meaningless shapes and colors arranged themselves and I saw a person, and blood. Lots of blood. My eyes went out of focus again and I dropped the picture. He handed me another one, a close up of Danielle's face, puffy and covered in brown blotches. I recognized her jawline, and her arm in the foreground of the photograph, bruised and blotchy, the fingers curled. One long nail hung broken, still attached by glue to a corner of the nail bed. The photographs had been taken in a hotel room: a lamp, a seascape screwed into the wall. In places brown blood obscured everything.

"It was a blunt instrument," he said. "It was heavy."

The next one showed her chest, pushed in and misshapen. Her fake boobs sat on top of the wrecked body, intact, pointing the wrong way. Blood soaked her blouse.

"Broken ribs," he said. "The bone shards punctured her lung. She could have died from that or the blood loss, we're still trying to determine that. Some of the injuries are postmortem. Do you understand what that means, Ms. Ford? The person who did this kept beating her after she was dead."

I closed my eyes and tried to breathe. My mouth flooded with saliva.

"You're not gonna throw up, are you?" he said.

He grabbed the wastebasket and set it down next to me. I gripped the table's edge and stood. I had to get out, get away from those pictures.

"I don't feel right," I said, but I couldn't hear myself because of the traffic sounds loud in my ears. I saw white.

When I regained consciousness I seemed to be lying on the floor. I couldn't hear. Nausea circled my body. The detective stood far above me, and I watched a uniformed cop hand him some brown paper towels and a cup of water. My head hurt. My arm hurt. I touched my head and my fingers came away wet.

"I don't think it's bad," the detective said to the other cop. "The head always bleeds a lot." He knelt beside me and said my name. "Ms. Ford? Charlotte? Can you focus on my hand? Follow my hand with your eyes."

His features were indistinct, backlit by the paneled lights in the ceiling. I tried to speak but the sounds scraped.

"I'm gonna sit you up, okay?" he said.

The detective lifted me by the shoulders while trying to support my head. He held the paper towels firmly to my brow, where it hurt the most. I blinked, leaning against him, and tried to focus my vision. He propped me against the wall and straightened my legs in front of me.

"Go get a soft drink," he told the other guy. "And a candy bar."

The detective took some clean paper towels from the pile next to me on the floor and replaced the bloody ones. I didn't mind sitting there while he took care of me. As long as I wasn't looking at those pictures anymore.

"It shouldn't need stitches," he said.

The other cop came in with a Hawaiian Punch and a bag of animal crackers. The detective popped the top on the can and held it to my lips. "Small sips, Charlotte. Good. You're all right, you'll be fine."

He lifted the towel from my face and said, "Your color's coming back. Put your arms around my neck. I think you can get up now. Ready? I'll help you."

I leaned into him. He smelled like rain and skin with sharp spice underneath. He eased me into the chair, took my hands, and placed them in my lap.

"You hit the table on your way down," he said. "Drink."

I took another sip of punch.

"We'll get you home soon, all right? You faint a lot?"

"No."

"If you feel dizzy, lean over. Rest your head between your knees. Don't get up so fast next time."

"Okay," I said.

"I'm sorry about the pictures. You all right now? Enough to talk?"

I nodded.

"Okay. You haven't seen Danielle lately, until Sunday."

"Yeah."

"Why Sunday?"

I took a deep ragged breath and began.

CHAPTER TWO

Detective Ash listened as I told him what happened Sunday. Danielle's mother Sally had called me that morning and insisted that I come by her office. I was surprised to hear from her. I didn't even know she had my number. But I heard the urgency in her voice and agreed to meet. I was curious, I guess. That, and I had nothing else to do. It was my day off from the coffee shop where I worked, and I'd thought I'd spend it with Michael, but he wasn't answering my texts.

Sally always was hard to say no to. I drove to her office building, a glass tower that rose in the Houston sky. Sally stepped outside and waved. She was dressed in tailored shorts, low mules, and a printed jersey blouse. Even in casual clothes she looked intimidating, rich.

"Hi, Charlotte," she said. "Thanks so much for stopping by."

"Sure," I said. I had always felt awkward around Sally. "It's no problem."

Our footsteps echoed over the polished stone surfaces to a bank of elevators. We went to her floor and she led me past a set of double doors, a reception desk, and a pair of leather couches. On the wall hung a series of photographs depicting various stages of the Rice Hotel revitalization project. Years ago, downtown was a deserted wasteland after five o'clock. No one believed that people might live there or go there at night. Sally's company had pioneered the downtown gentrification, changed the city, and made millions. Now urban lofts sprouted everywhere, even in the suburbs.

The air-conditioning froze my sweat, and goose bumps rose along my arms. We walked down the hall to her office. A huge window overlooked the building's atrium, filled with large leafy plants, ferns, and birds of paradise. Filtered sunlight fell in patches on the sleek office furniture. "Have a seat," she said, indicating a pair of plush chairs. We each took one.

"How are you, sweetie?" she said. "How's school going?"

"I'm taking this semester off," I said. "Taking a break."

"I wish Danielle had gone to college," Sally said. "She never has done things the regular way."

"I guess not," I said.

"How is Danielle, anyhow?" She tried to sound casual. Soft lines showed around her eyes and mouth.

"Good, I guess. We don't really hang out."

Sally nodded. "I haven't seen her since before she . . . left," she said.

I ignored Sally's clumsy euphemism for prison. I wasn't surprised Danielle had stayed away from her. She and Sally had never been close.

"Charlotte, I need her phone number."

"You don't have it?" I said, surprised.

"She changed it. I have the old one, from when she was on my cell phone plan. We haven't talked in a long time."

I did know how to get in touch with Danielle—we'd run into each other at a restaurant a couple of months back and exchanged numbers. But if Danielle wanted to avoid Sally, no way was I getting in the middle of it. I frowned, looking out the window. So strange to see all the tropical plants growing indoors. It seemed backwards.

"Charlotte, I know this puts you in an awkward position. But I really need your help. I need to get ahold of her. My aunt died."

"Gosh," I said. "I'm sorry."

"Well, she'd been ill a long time. The problem is, she left Danielle an inheritance. Now the probate lawyers need to talk to her, there's paperwork to do, and she's nowhere to be found. It's a bit embarrassing."

She said this last in a whisper, leaning forward, conspiratorial.

"Please help me," she said. As she spoke she slid a white envelope over to me.

"What's this?" I said.

"Open it."

Inside the envelope was a sheaf of hundred-dollar bills. I counted them twice—a thousand dollars.

"I know you can use it," Sally said. "I just need her phone number. Please."

There was no way I could pass up that much money. I searched through my phone for Danielle's number and read it off to Sally.

"Perfect, darling, thank you so much. I'll call her tonight, as soon as I'm finished up here."

"Thank you," I said. "For the money."

She stood. "Oh, sweetie. It's been lovely to see you. You get prettier and prettier. Can you find your way out?"

"Yeah, sure," I said.

She hugged me goodbye, smothering me again in her expensive perfume, her aura of wealth and power. I hurried past the smooth stone walls of the lobby and out to the parking lot, with its clean painted lines slanting in parallels. I sat in my hot car for a minute, letting my skin thaw before turning the ignition. I felt dazed by the heat and the money in my pocket.

I texted Danielle immediately. *It's Charlotte. Have to see you. It's important. Drink?* She texted me back and we made plans to meet at six at a new bar called the Mockingbird.

Later I drove through traffic to the bar, which occupied a corner strip mall on Westheimer, along with a dry cleaners, one window-broken vacancy, and an accountant's office called Tax Mex. Inside I ignored the cheap specials and ordered Maker's, rocks; I was rich. Danielle showed up late, when I was on my second drink. She was gorgeous, as always, but in a weird, doll-like way: long streaked hair, too much makeup. Her tits looked bigger, fake.

"Charlotte, wow," she said. "It's nice to see you." She gave me a half hug, kissed the air near my cheek.

"You look great," I said.

"Thanks. So do you."

She ordered a peach martini from the bartender and I got another whiskey.

"So what's going on?" she said.

"Don't get upset."

"Uh-oh, Charlotte, what?"

"Your mom paid me a thousand dollars for your phone number," I said.

"What?"

"Yeah." I handed her Sally's envelope. "Here's your half."

She opened the flap and thumbed through the bills. "You gave her my number?" she said.

"Yeah. Because she gave me *a thousand dollars.*"

"Does she want me to have this?"

"She doesn't know."

Danielle squinted at me. "Then why are you giving it to me?"

"I figured, worst-case scenario, you could use it to get a new phone. It felt weird to keep it and not warn you."

"Thanks."

"Free money, right? Why not."

She set the envelope on the bar and centered her drink on top of it. A sticky pink ring dampened the paper.

"Fucking Sally," she said.

"I know."

"She's ridiculous."

"I know," I said. "I would have given up your digits for a lot less."

"Shut up," Danielle said, laughing.

"Has she called you yet?"

"No. What does she want?"

"She wants to tell you your great-aunt died."

"Aunt Baby? God, we used to go to her place when I was little. She lived out in Tomball."

"She left you something in her will. You'll have to see the lawyer and sign papers, I guess."

"God, Sally *and* her lawyer? The worst."

"I'm sorry about your aunt."

Danielle shrugged. "I barely remember her. Still, it's sad. Anyways. It's great to see you. What have you been doing all this time? I'm surprised we haven't run into each other more."

"I guess I stay in the neighborhood a lot. I've been working at Common Grounds on Shepherd. The coffee shop."

"Oh, I know that place. I never go in there. So what else? Are you seeing anybody?"

I laughed. "All you care about is boys," I said. "But yes,

yeah, I have a boyfriend. He's in a band, he's nice, we've been together about a year."

"Is it serious?"

"I don't know, maybe. Kind of serious, yeah. How about you? How've you been?"

She rested her hand on the edge of the bar. I'd forgotten her grace, her perfect posture. Her wrists were delicate and freckled.

"I'm doing okay. Good, actually. It really is nice to see you. I can finally have a chance to say thank you for your letters."

I'd written to her in prison but never heard back.

"I wondered if you got them," I said.

"I got them. It was really nice of you. They cheered me up."

"Was it awful in there?" I asked. "I'm so sorry you had to go through all that."

"It was, yeah. I don't want to talk about it. But it was good in some ways, too. I got clean. It's been almost three years."

"That's great. I'm so glad," I said.

"I wanted to write you back," she said. "It was NA. They really pressure you to cut ties with the people you did drugs with. To make it easier to kick."

"It's okay," I said. "I mean, whatever helps, right?"

"Yeah."

We sipped our drinks for a minute.

"So what else have you been up to?" I said. "Since you got out?"

"First thing I did was go on a diet. I got fat in there."

"You did not. I don't believe it."

"It's true!" Danielle said. "They gave us mashed potatoes every fucking day. I gained like five pounds."

"Oh no, five pounds." I rolled my eyes.

"Charlotte, listen. I'm glad you texted me."

"Well, of course. How could I not?"

"No, I mean I missed you. A lot. I know I screwed things up."

"No more than me," I said, flustered. "You had bad luck, getting caught. I've missed you, too."

"You're so sweet," she said, putting her arm around me.

"We went through a lot of shit together. I'm glad you're doing okay now."

"Me, too," she said, turning to kiss me on the cheek.

A slim, dark-haired girl came up behind us. She looked about our age, mid-twenties, and pretty. Her lips twisted in a half smile.

"Aww, you guys are adorable," the girl said.

"Audrey, hey," Danielle said, letting go of me. "Charlotte, this is my friend Audrey."

I felt both relieved and irritated at the interruption.

"Hi," I said. "It's nice to meet you."

"You, too," Audrey said.

"Charlotte is my oldest, dearest friend," Danielle said. "We haven't seen each other in ages. We have to catch up."

"How about a drink?" Audrey said. "Another round?"

"Sure," Danielle said.

Audrey ordered whiskey, same as me. The bartender brought our drinks, sloshing Danielle's martini as he set it down.

Danielle turned to me. "Did you hear about Joey?" she said.

"No," I said.

"He got locked up. Out west. New Mexico, I think."

"Who's Joey?" Audrey asked.

"My boyfriend from before," Danielle said. "We used to, when we'd fuck, we used to try to come at the same time, and right at that second we would shoot each other up. I thought we'd get married. I never had anything like that with anybody else."

"That's insane," Audrey said. "You're insane."

"I loved him," Danielle said. "Fuck, I loved him. We were so in love it was crazy."

"Are you serious?" Audrey said. "Yeah, that's fucking crazy!"

"We were fucking romantic," Danielle said. She rubbed a mark on her French manicure. She was definitely getting tipsy. Showing off a little, too. I couldn't tell if she was trying to impress me or Audrey. Maybe both of us.

"Tell me," I said, "how do y'all two know each other?"

"From work," Audrey said.

"Don't tell her," Danielle said to Audrey.

"Don't tell me what?" I said.

"Yeah, don't tell her what?" Audrey said.

"You'll freak out," Danielle said to me.

"No, she won't," Audrey said. "You're being paranoid."

"Fine," Danielle said. "There's this guy named Brandon, he works at the cable access channel, Mediasource. He's a film-maker and he does programming and stuff. We work with him on private projects. We're models."

"She's so weird about it," Audrey said. "We're not models, but they call it modeling. It's for a porn site. Videos."

"You're porn stars?"

"We're not *stars*," Danielle said.

"Speak for yourself," Audrey said.

She tossed her hair and pursed her lips, arching her back in a pinup pose. I laughed.

"Wow," I said. "How does it work? You fuck people and there's a camera?"

"See?" Danielle said to Audrey. "She's freaking out."

"I'm not freaking out," I said.

And I wasn't. I wasn't even surprised.

"What's it like?" I asked Audrey.

"It's a job. It's work. There's a lot of waiting around, stopping and starting. The guys take forever. Or the Viagra wears off."

"Yeah," Danielle said. "And you have to look perfect no matter what."

"You have to try not to look bored," Audrey said. "Even though it's really boring. Mostly, anyway."

"It's easier than dancing," Danielle said. "At least you always get paid."

"Plus Brandon's nice," Audrey said.

"Yeah, he's not a douche bag like you'd think," Danielle said. "He also makes art movies. He's super talented."

"You should come to his screening," Audrey said. "He's showing one of his experimental films next week. There'll be a reception. Free booze."

"Sounds cool," I said. "What's the website called?"

"Can we talk about something else, please?" Danielle said.

"Come on," I said.

"SweetDreamz," Audrey said. "With a Z. SweetDreamz.net."

"It's a dumb name," Danielle said.

"So what?" Audrey said.

"I am totally looking it up as soon as I get home," I said, teasing.

"Come on, don't," Danielle said.

"Oh my god," I said. "I'm kidding, I'm kidding. I won't."

"You should, though," Audrey said.

Danielle rolled her eyes. "Enough. We have to go. We're meeting people for dinner."

I wondered if she was running away from the conversation. I decided not to bring up her job next time we met.

"Well, it's great to see you," I said.

"Me, too," Danielle said. "This was fun. I'll see you at the screening?"

"Sure," I said. "Text me the details."

Audrey rose and smiled.

"Bye," she said. "It was nice meeting you."

Danielle got up, swinging her handbag onto her shoulder. She left the envelope of cash on the bar.

"Hey, you're forgetting this," I said, picking it up. It was soggy with condensation from her glass.

"Keep it," she said.

"No. That's nuts."

"I don't need it. I don't want anything from *her*."

I recognized the tone she reserved for Sally, full of contempt. I knew her well enough to let the subject drop. I nodded, put the envelope in my bag, and waved goodbye. At least I'd tried. Not that I minded keeping the cash. Danielle was always weird about money. I guess it means something different when you grow up rich.

In the dank concrete police station Detective Ash asked me questions. As long as I kept talking he seemed pleased, and I didn't have to think about those photographs in the manila folder. As long as I kept talking, Danielle seemed alive.

"What was she doing in that motel room?" Ash said.

"I don't know."

"Was she seeing anybody?"

"She didn't mention anyone."

"Who did she meet at the motel?"

"I don't know," I said. "I told you everything she said."

"Was she turning tricks?" he said.

"What?" I said.

He regarded me with this patient unwavering gaze, oddly intimate.

"I don't know," I said.

"Did she ever do anything like that before?"

"Sort of," I said.

"Tell me about that."

"This was years ago," I said. "We were like nineteen."

"Okay."

"She had a job dancing at Dolls. This regular at the club, this rich guy, he was really into her. He offered her two thousand dollars to spend the night with him."

"What happened?"

"She did it. It was a lot of money. And he was nice. She liked him, too. I mean, she knew him, it's not like he was a stranger."

"What was his name?" he said.

"Tom, Tim, maybe. I can't remember."

"Where did they spend the night?" he said.

"A fancy hotel. He was rich."

"Was that the only time?"

"No, she saw him again. A few times, I guess. It didn't seem dangerous. Danielle felt like she'd pulled off a scam, in a way. All that cash in one night—she said it was easy."

I remembered thinking it wasn't that big a deal. I might have done the same thing, if I'd had the opportunity.

"Were there others?" he said.

"I don't know," I said. "We stopped hanging out."

"How did she get along with her mother?" he said.

"She didn't. Danielle hated Sally."

He waited for me to say more. I hesitated. Even if she was dead, they were still her secrets.

"Talk to me, Charlotte. You're helping Danielle by talking to me."

His hand touched my arm. His warmth in the cold room felt like a terrible kindness.

"Sally expected Danielle to go to some fancy school and join the Junior League or whatever. Danielle wasn't interested in that world."

The detective nodded, made some notes.

"What else?" he said.

"Isn't that enough?" I said.

"You tell me."

"Sally worked all the time. She was never around. They weren't close, that's all."

He kept me there a while longer, asking question after question, repeating himself. I went through the same information three, four times. I was too tired to cry. And finally, it ended. He called to the other cop, who walked me out to a squad car. Ash stood by the building with his arms at his sides while bugs danced under the yellow streetlight. It had stopped raining. The police car smelled of old socks, dirty plastic. I stared out the window the whole way home.

CHAPTER THREE

By morning the city was hot and muggy, awash in dirty yellow air. I changed clothes and went for a run. I headed towards the museum district, where buildings of cool stone rose from the ground. I followed the crushed granite trail behind the zoo, circling the park, passing the man-made pond. I jumped over steaming puddles and jogged home through the neighborhood, brushing the elephant ear begonias that draped over the sidewalk. Some of the broad leaves sagged, broken by the heavy rains. Sweat soaked my clothes. I ran fast, trying not to think, but I couldn't keep Danielle out of my head.

We had first met freshman year of high school, at the movie theater where we both worked. She stole money from the box office, which we used to buy weed from the projectionist. We smoked on the roof, crouched behind the big R of the theater sign. We could see the Galleria and Memorial Park, could turn in a circle and follow the Loop from the mall to the Astrodome, north to the Heights, the whole green tree-lined city, almost scenic. The roof, not the cash or the pot, kept us at that dismal job for nearly a year.

We hung out at Danielle's house, which we often had to our-selves. Sally worked long hours, and Danielle and I pilfered her liquor and swam in the pool. I felt so lucky to be Danielle's friend. She was funny and beautiful. We talked about every-thing.

I hated it when Sally came home. She and Danielle always fought, and I hid in Danielle's room or read magazines in the pool house, played music loud to drown out the yelling. Even worse, Sally went out of her way to be nice to me, which hurt Danielle's feelings. It was weird all the way around. Still, I liked it better than my place. We had only three rooms, and my mom was always home.

Danielle was easily the coolest girl at our school. She wore outfits no one else could pull off—scarves and hats and glam-orous upswept hair. She dressed for class like a movie star at some gala, and it seemed elegant, never pretentious. Sometimes being around her made me feel sparkly, too. But other times I felt like nothing next to her. Whatever I did, she would do it louder, sexier. If a boy liked me, Danielle would come around, bright and silly, and he couldn't help but be into her instead. It wasn't her fault. She was like candy, irresistible. A glow came off her.

She was good to me in ways that mattered. Back in mid-dle school and high school everyone assumed my mom was a junkie. Not just kids, the teachers, too. I could see the judg-ment in their faces. But they didn't understand that my mom was sick. She took medicine to help with the pain and keep her calm. The doctors were always running tests and giving her new prescriptions. They never figured out what was wrong, but that didn't make it any less real. She couldn't work, couldn't get through a day without an attack of pain so acute it left her unable to stand.

Danielle didn't care what the other kids said. She and my mom got along, too, the few times Danielle came over. Danielle treated her like a person, never acted scared or weirded out, even when my mom was so sick or zonked on meds that she couldn't speak. After my mom died, Danielle helped me clean the apartment. She threw out a bunch of junk and repainted the walls while I was in a daze of grief. She brought me presents: throw pillows for the couch, posters, a set of matching dishes. Eventually she moved in.

As I cleaned out my mother's things I found pill bottles all over the place, in cabinets and drawers, in the pockets of her sweaters. Demerol, Xanax, Percocet, Oxycontin. It was senior year, and my mom was dead. We had parties.

The pills kept coming, automatic refills from my mom's mail-order pharmacy. Massive amounts of them. Danielle and I started selling them to friends, friends of friends, kids from school. We made plenty of money, enough to pay the rent and bills and not have to work. It went on like that for nearly a year. When the drugs dried up I felt relieved, like my mom had finally finished dying.

I actually liked being sober, having energy again. I enrolled in a few classes at the community college and got a new restaurant job. But Danielle loved getting high. After the pills were gone she started snorting heroin. At first it didn't seem that different—just one more drug to try. But Danielle changed when she started shooting up. The dope made her slow and vacant, no fun to talk to. Soon all she thought about was getting high. I knew it was my fault, that my mom's pills got her addicted.

I tried to help her. I gave her rides to the methadone clinic, I encouraged her. She would lie to me, say she was clean, but I would come home from school to find her sweating and shaking, and I'd know she had a fever from a dirty batch. She couldn't quit.

Seeing Danielle like that, nodding, her eyes glazed, her arms bruised—it scared me. She'd get high and drink Cokes and suck on hard candies, letting the plastic wrappers fall as she nodded in and out, idly scratching her arm. Those wrappers littered every room. Eventually Sally found out and quit giving her money. Maybe Sally thought that would make it easier for Danielle to kick, if she had to get a job and go to work every day. But Danielle started dancing and all those girls were doing drugs, too.

One night I went out with friends from work and drank too much tequila. I could hardly move the next morning, for the nausea and pain. In the kitchen I poured a ginger ale and began searching for aspirin.

"You poor baby," Danielle said. "Why don't you try this. Come on, it's a painkiller. Your headache will go away."

Still drunk, I assented and let her tie a scarf around my arm. I was grateful for her touch. I'd missed her. She slid the needle in with such care. To be the focus of her attention—it was the best feeling, until the dope hit, and then *that* was the best feeling. For a few minutes I cared about nothing, held in a soft, swirling cloud, until the swirling part took over and I vomited for half an hour. My headache returned, more intense than before. Danielle hardly noticed because she was high, too. I did heroin a few more times after that. I was trying to keep up with her, trying to be with her, but it was never any fun for me. Soon she hooked up with Joey and moved out. And then she went to prison, twenty-four months for possession.

After seeing her on Sunday, I had thought we would be friends again. I kept accidentally thinking that way, and then I remembered she was dead. My mind was going in circles:

it didn't make sense, it couldn't be real, she was fine, I'd just seen her. It felt like I could call her up and she'd answer and I could tell her about the police station. She would laugh about me fainting, we would turn it into a funny story, an inside joke, part of our shared history.

I sat at the computer and typed in Danielle's website, Sweet Dreamz.net. I did it without really knowing why. Maybe I just wanted to see her.

A dozen close-up photos of girls were displayed on a pink grid. You could click on each one to watch a teaser or pay eighteen dollars to get the whole video. I saw an image of Danielle. Hair in pigtails, she leaned forward to show her cleavage. I clicked on her picture and it went to a video clip, twenty seconds of her squatting in stilettos, rubbing her shaved pussy and pinching her nipples, fingernails flashing in the studio light. She looked into the camera and moaned. "$17.95" flashed on the screen and Danielle said, "I'm so-o wet. I need to get fucked."

I clicked on another video, with Danielle and Audrey together. Danielle bent at the waist, licking and squeezing Audrey's tits. They were smaller than Danielle's and obviously real, with long brown nipples. Danielle's ass bounced in the foreground, and Audrey wailed, her face contorted. The image cut to the price screen again, and a man's voice said, "Hot lesbian sluts. Watch these sluts come!" Another clip showed Audrey being fucked from behind, pounded by a guy, her eyes dazed and huge, her nipples erect.

The videos embarrassed me and I wished I hadn't watched them. I was sad and turned on, and irritated that I could be aroused by something so tacky. I was mad at myself for watching, for being such a perv. What would I tell Danielle next time I saw her? And then I remembered that she was dead.

I slammed the laptop shut and tossed it aside. I was crying again. I had to get out of the apartment, be around people. I needed whiskey. Several whiskeys. I texted my boyfriend Michael, *I need a drink. Meet me?* He wrote back, *At Harp, come on.*

I would tell Michael about Danielle, I would cry while he held me and tried to comfort me. And once that happened, I knew it would seem real. I rode my bike to the Harp, a pub housed in a ramshackle bungalow. I pushed through the crowd to the wooden bar. Pockmarks distorted the neon reflection along its length. Michael sat on a stool in the corner, looking at his phone. The bartender brought my whiskey and I took a long sip. I went over to him.

"Hey," I said.

"Hi, baby," he said. He smiled weakly, and I saw that he was very drunk, barely balanced on his stool.

"How long have you been here?" I asked.

"I don't know. Let's get another round."

"You get it. I'm going outside," I said.

The noise and the air-conditioning and the crowd were too much for me. I could feel tears already burning my eyes. I found an empty picnic table on the patio. This corner near the building was dark, away from the streetlights. Finally Michael stumbled outside, carrying two whiskeys. He sat across from me on the opposite bench and took a cigarette from my pack. I lit it for him. I'd rarely seen him smoke. I lit one for myself, too.

"Charlotte, we have to talk," he said.

"Yeah," I said. "Something happened."

He looked at me strangely. "How'd you know?" he said.

"What do you mean?"

I wanted him to see that I was upset and put his arms around me, but he was too drunk, he wasn't paying attention. He took a deep breath, looked away from me.

"I saw Sonja," he said.

"So what." Sonja was his ex. I knew she worked at the art supply store and lived nearby. I saw her around the neighborhood sometimes, too. I didn't care about her or whatever gossip she had told him. Danielle was dead. Who gave a fuck about Sonja?

"We . . ." he started and stopped. "Charlotte, I'm sorry," he tried again. "You know I love you. I respect you. I know this isn't fair."

"What isn't?" I said slowly.

"I slept with her," he said.

I thought of Sonja's long red hair, her pale freckled arms. I'd always thought she was way prettier than me.

"I didn't plan it," he said. "It just sort of happened."

I couldn't think properly. I felt stunned, slow. I was glad we were outside in the dark. I didn't want him to see my face while he was saying these things.

"I ran into her at a show. At Rudyard's. We got to talking and it was like—like old times, I guess. Charlotte, I'm really sorry."

A question occurred to me. "When?" I said. "When did you sleep with her?"

"It was like a month ago."

"Jesus, Michael."

"I know, I know, I should have told you earlier."

"You should have told me? You should have never done it!"

"I know, you're right."

"Just that one time?"

"Well . . ."

"You've been fucking her for a month? How many times?"

"I don't see why that matters."

"Where? At her place?"

He shrugged, miserably.

"Oh, at your place? In your bed? Where I've slept, like hundreds of times?"

"I'm sorry," he said.

"Are you going to see her again?" I said.

"I'm not explaining this very well," Michael said.

"Then explain it better," I said.

"I'm going back with her. We're back together. I can't see you anymore."

I felt the words before I understood their meaning. It was a physical feeling, a dizziness and a pain in my stomach. I flinched.

"You're great," he was saying. "You'll find someone, I know you will. Don't take it personally, okay?"

"Don't take it personally? Fuck you."

"Charlotte, please."

"No," I said, loud. "Stop it."

I was trying not to cry. I drank, not looking at him. A stream of cars passed, fluttering the trash in the gutter. Someone tossed a cigarette from a driver's-side window. It hit the street in a bouquet of sparks.

"Charlotte, we can still be friends. Sonja wouldn't mind. I care about you. That hasn't changed. Maybe after a while we could all hang out. I think you'd like her."

"Sonja wouldn't mind?"

"All I mean is, I don't want to lose you. We had some good times, you know?"

He was wasted, slurring. That made me mad, that he had gotten drunk before he could tell me. That he couldn't do it sober. Maybe he had been drinking with her before I came to meet him. I felt anger, but also an unexpected gratitude. This pain was better, more manageable than my grief over Danielle.

I was thankful for the distraction. Even so, I couldn't listen to him anymore. I got up to leave. He put his arm out, reached for me, and I knocked him away. The contact energized me and I shoved him. It felt good so I did it again.

"You asshole," I said. My voice sounded cold.

He grabbed me and tried to hug me, but I pushed him away. I left. I didn't say another word, didn't look at him. I went over to my bike, unlocked it, and rode unsteadily over the cracked sidewalk to the street. At the corner I turned off Richmond and crossed the neighborhood to the bayou. It was buggy along there. The water was still pretty high and I could hear it rushing. The trail was smooth and dark and abandoned, except for hovering clouds of gnats. I rode as fast as I could until my legs were tired and I didn't feel anything anymore and the last few days seemed like something I might have imagined.

CHAPTER FOUR

When I woke dressed in yesterday's clothes, it was eight o'clock already. I was late for my shift. The café had called three times. I dressed quickly and made it there by eight thirty.

"I'm sorry," I said to Andrew, the manager, who was steaming a pitcher of soy milk.

"Jesus, Charlotte. You were scheduled for two hours ago. Did you even brush your hair?"

I started to respond but he'd already turned to a waiting customer.

"I've got a meeting," he said to me. "Take over. We can talk about this later."

In the next hour and a half I dropped two drinks and accidentally gave three people regular instead of decaf. I spilled the bottle of vanilla syrup onto the black mat, which meant I'd have to spend my break washing the mat and the floor so it wouldn't draw ants. My coworker Jessie suggested that I work the register instead. I shook my head. I knew if I had to make eye contact with anyone I would cry. Around eleven I had time to drag the mat to the floor drain in the back and hose it down. I covered Jessie's break up front, and sucked down an espresso and half a cigarette before the lunch rush. At two my shift ended. My whole body felt sore and sticky, and my head throbbed. I drove home.

I took the whiskey bottle down from the top of the fridge. A pill of dust clung to the bottle, drifted to the floor. I had a brief vision in which I saw myself bring a chair to the kitchen, stand on it, and wipe the refrigerator with a rag and soapy water. I was too exhausted to do it.

I ran a bath and took the whiskey bottle into the tub. Hot water inched up the sides of my breasts, rising with each exhale. I lay not thinking, heat radiating through me, pumping into the heart and out, to my limbs, my fingertips. I sipped the whiskey. Let me stay like this, I thought—clean. It was almost a prayer, but to no one. The water covered me, and the temperature reached equilibrium, making my whole body blank and warm. There was nothing, now, to feel or do.

I thought about the dust on top of the fridge, and other dust that I couldn't see—fan blades, window frames. I imagined I could hear it gathering, a tiny army collecting its troops. When my mom was alive the house was always dusty, a mess everywhere, especially around her favorite chair. On bad days she might accidentally knock over a glass of Diet Coke and not even clean it up. Right now I could relate. I got out of the bath, wrapped a towel around my head, and fell into bed, exhausted. I suppose I was drunk, though I couldn't tell. A bird and a squirrel fought on a maple branch outside my window. They shrieked and chattered. I let sleep overtake me, glad for it.

I dreamt of Danielle. We were in a school bathroom together and she tried to show me how to shoot heroin into a

vein on my forehead because that was how you were supposed
to do it with this needle shaped like a knife. It was a new kind
of needle that was safer and more effective. I had to look in
the mirror while I did it. In the dream I got high and thought,
Oh! Finally.

I woke in early evening, groaning, and staggered to the
bathroom to throw up. I wished I could sleep backwards. To
last week, last year, four years ago. Danielle and I should have
skipped town, moved to Austin or Portland, someplace better.
But Danielle, she'd been with Joey. She wouldn't have gone
with me anyway. Now it was too late. She was dead, Danielle
was dead. I felt so tired.

I brushed my teeth, dressed in a miniskirt and high-heeled
sandals with ankle straps. I fixed my makeup and hair and
drove to the bar. I needed to be around people and think about
something else. Maybe someone would be kind to me.

The leftover happy-hour crowd mingled with the kids stopping in for their first drink. I took a seat at the bar. A man
in office clothes tried to hit on this girl in a green dress. She
giggled, clearly embarrassed. I ordered a Manhattan. A few
minutes later they were kissing sloppily. What did he say to
her, I wondered.

A guy edged between me and the next barstool.

"Can I buy you a drink?" he said.

I studied him. He was cute, in a fratty way, his boy-band
hair gelled into place. I didn't mind having someone to talk to.
I smiled.

"Okay," I said.

"I'm Peter," he said.

"I'm Eliza," I lied. What did it matter?

"I love the name Eliza," he said.

"Me, too," I said.

"You like this song?"

"I guess." I hadn't been paying attention to the music.

"Dance with me," he said.

"Maybe later," I said. Nobody danced in this bar. Who was this guy?

I thought of Danielle before her arrest. When she first started stripping she danced constantly. Even high, she couldn't sit still. She would dance across the room to switch on a lamp.

The boy, Peter, gestured to the bartender for a round.

"So," he said. "Are you in fashion?"

"Sorry?"

"That's what my friend and I thought. Either that or a singer, a performer of some type. Are you like a singer?"

"I work at a hospital," I lied.

"Wow, I would never have guessed." To his credit he didn't look disappointed.

"I'm in school," he said. "I'm a business major. I'll be graduating this summer."

"That's great," I said, not caring.

"Let's go sit on the couch."

That prospect held little appeal. The couch was made of an extremely porous material soaked nightly in smoke and sweat and beer. Peter took my arm, and I saw the matter had been decided. I gathered my cigarettes, my lighter, my new drink. It seemed I would not be able to manage my sprawl of small possessions. The couch enveloped us.

I felt okay. I felt better. Later, I felt great. I didn't need Michael, I could do okay on my own. I was drunk enough not to care about anything outside the press of bodies around me and the pressure of his hand. In the middle of these people I was in a private space. Peter was making it all right. I could hand myself over, and the world could be happy and he would want me and I would be okay.

The sun was setting, another lovely pollution-stained sky. I gazed out the window while he nuzzled my neck. As I watched, the electric colors filled the world so full I was afraid it might burst. Reds, oranges. I longed to be part of it. I was inside a dark bar with someone's hand on my leg when I should have been in the sunset. In the sky. But there I was on the couch, helpless, dazzled.

I raised my eyes to the TV above the window, which played a commercial for shower cleaner. Animated scrub brushes sped over blue tile, leaving sparkles in their wake. Peter's hand raised goose bumps along my arms. He proposed a toast and we clinked glass to bottle. I smiled, glad to exist in this window of possibility, before it got usurped by waste and disappointment. The mix of chemicals in my blood danced and settled, danced and settled. Pink streaks glowed on the surfaces in the room. All the bad that happened in the world gave urgency to their beauty. Soon the sunset colors vanished, and it was dark and smelly where I was. I made an effort to focus on the boy. He was talking about his new apartment. I tried to participate.

"Where do you live again?" I asked.

"Meyerland."

"Outside the Loop?" I said.

"Not far outside. It gets free Wi-Fi."

He was boring, but I didn't mind, because his attention was interesting.

"We need another drink," I said, and stood.

He went to the bar, more crowded now, and I moved closer to the television. A closed caption *Law & Order* gave way to the local news: a Hispanic girl with big eyes took turns looking cheerful and serious. I tried to read her lips but I could only read her eyes. They were empty and anxious despite the emotions moving across the rest of her face. The picture jumped to a River Oaks street, broad and landscaped, and a flash of Sally's face. The Hispanic girl came on again and then another set of commercials. The boy installed a fresh drink in my hand and I sipped it and waited through cat food and sitcom ads until the news came on again. The screen went to Sally, standing in her backyard. Her face was made up, with tears carefully placed, flattering her features. She looked like Danielle. Almost young. A somber-faced handsome reporter was holding a microphone. Captions ran at the bottom of the screen: "gruesome slaying."

I'd spent countless nights in that backyard, swimming in the pool, smoking weed on the lounge chairs. It was odd to see it on TV, with the volume muted. I watched, glad it had turned into a TV show. That meant I could turn it off.

"Eliza. Eliza."

I'd forgotten I was Eliza. The boy had been trying to get my attention. His friend was there, too.

"Eliza, hey. We're gonna go outside for a minute. Come on, come with us."

I gulped my drink and set it on the bar. Outside we huddled between a Suburban and an Escalade. The size of the cars was screwing with my perspective. I felt like a fiberglass statue, realistic but hollow, smaller than life. I took one hit off the bowl and held it, and when I tried to light a cigarette I couldn't even get it to my mouth.

"What is this shit?" I asked them. Both boys giggled.

"Good, right?" his friend said.

The event of him speaking packaged itself and retreated forever. I hadn't heard him so much as just knew what he had said. It was like I just *knew*. Amazing.

"It's California shit. The Mexi-schwag around here gives me a headache. I can't smoke it anymore. Look at this—" I understood he wanted to show me something. "See the crystals, the way it reflects? Pure THC."

"Oh," I said. "You're very proud."

"Dude, don't hold it like that! People might see."

This must have been Peter speaking. I couldn't see him but I could determine his rough location, from the lack of negative space. I felt clever for the way I was keeping track. It wasn't easy trying to hear through the space separating us. I got the cigarette lit and immediately the parking lot pitched and lurched. I couldn't hear the two boys anymore, I lost them. I couldn't find the cars. I couldn't find the TV anywhere, and this made me very, very sad.

Broken glass in the asphalt under my hands shone here and there, like the crystals in the bud. I crouched near a weedy fence, dandelion leaves jagged at the base of the chain link. I hooked my fingers through the links and pulled myself up.

I was pleased to see the door to the bar not too far away. I knew I could get there if I concentrated. I felt very cold. Was it cold? What month was it? Wasn't it spring? I approached the door, but got scared of going in. The next second I forgot that, and opened the door. I couldn't see very well and I wondered if my contacts had fallen out. I found a stool at the bar and leaned against it, undignified. I tried to hold still and not smile.

"Charlotte. What can I get you?" Eric, the bartender: what an amazing coincidence, to see him again.

"Hi!" I said.

"Are you doing all right, kid? What do you need?"

I considered his questions and answered truthfully. "I don't know," I said.

He nodded and left and I forgot about him. He suddenly appeared again with a glass of water and a bag of Fritos. He left them on the bar in front of me. I attacked the bag of chips. I heard Michael laugh behind me. I loved Michael's laugh. I turned towards the sound, smiling. That's how stoned I was: I heard Michael and smiled. Then I remembered, and I saw him in a group of people at a table near the pinball machine. His fingers entwined in a mass of orange hair attached to *her*, Sonja. I dropped the Fritos on the bar and walked over to their table.

"Hi, Sonja," I said. My voice sounded strange and bright, chirpy.

They both looked up.

"Charlotte," Michael said. "What do you want?"

"I'm not talking to you," I said. "I wanted to say hi to your new girlfriend, that's all."

"Hi," Sonja said. "It's nice to meet you."

"Is it?" I said. "Is it nice?"

"Come on, Charlotte, don't do this," Michael said. "We're trying to have a drink, okay?"

"Fuck you," I said, not looking at him. "You don't get to talk to me anymore. Leave us alone."

"Charlotte, I'm really sorry," Sonja said. "I know this must be very hard for you. I never intended for any of it to happen."

"Sorry for what?" I said. "What are you sorry for? Specifically."

"Um . . ."

"Charlotte, leave her alone."

"Look, she's afraid to say why. Or ashamed. Are you ashamed

of yourself, Sonja? You're so pretty. No wonder he wants to fuck you."

I reached out and stroked her long hair. She flinched at my touch.

"You must have missed him when we were together," I said.

"I guess."

She looked terrified. I was glad.

"You know he's a liar, though, right?" I said.

"Charlotte, come on, stop it."

"No, Michael, she should know this. I mean, she might not be smart enough to put it together. Isn't that what you used to say about her? That she was too naïve? You couldn't stand always having to protect her and explain things to her? She was like a child? It made him impatient," I said to her. "He told me all about why he dumped you."

"I think we should leave," she said to Michael.

"Wait," I said. "I thought you should keep in mind that for a month—an entire month—he was fucking both of us and I had no idea. He's very good at keeping secrets, aren't you, Michael? Doesn't it make you wonder what he's not telling you?"

Michael stood up. "Okay, that's enough," he said. He stepped between us. "We're leaving. Go back to your table or whatever. Leave her alone."

He put his hand on my arm, trying to steer me away from her. Under his hand my nerve endings bunched in protest.

"Don't touch me," I said.

"Charlotte, quit yelling," Michael said. Still, he took his hand away. Sonja was standing up now, too, holding her purse and edging away from us. She looked stricken and pale.

"Go wait in the car," he said to Sonja.

"I thought you wanted to be friends," I said. I was about to cry.

Suddenly, magically, Peter appeared at my side.

"Eliza! There you are. Is this guy bothering you?"

"No," Michael said. "Who the fuck are you?"

"I think you should leave," Peter said. He was doing some kind of macho posturing with his hands on his hips, leaning towards Michael. It cheered me up immensely. I smiled at Peter. I liked being saved. More people should save me. I would like to be saved all the time.

"She's not interested, fella," Peter said.

Michael shook his head. "Y'all have a great night," he said, disgusted. He went to the front door.

"I have your stuff," Peter said. "You left it on the couch."

I squinted at my purse, my phone, my pink sweater. I felt his fingers on my neck.

"When you touch me," I said, "the room swims."

"Who were those people?"

"Nobody. Are they gone?"

"Yeah. Want another drink?"

"No, let's go back outside."

Outside we smoked some more weed and he pushed me against somebody's truck and kissed my neck until I shivered. I loved this part. Sex was so simple. I could give him what he wanted without having to worry about doing something wrong. He fumbled with the buttons of my blouse. The jukebox got louder as someone opened the door to the bar. After a while we decided to leave and Peter went in to close his tab. I tried to remember if I had brought the car or ridden my bike or what. I couldn't see the cars very well, not until I got close enough to touch each vehicle. I groped from one to another, squinting at each truck and sedan to see if I recognized it. Not that finding the car would do any good—my keys were trapped inside my bag. I would never manage to get them out. They were as remote as winter. I gave up and turned away from the yellow Volvo I'd been leaning against. Peter came outside and put his arm around me. He walked me to a red car and unlocked it with a button in his hand.

"Get in," he said.

CHAPTER FIVE

In the car Peter told a story about how one of his friends set a fire in a park. He meant it to be a funny story, but I had trouble following it because the lights on the road kept getting in my eyes. Red lights and white lights, and the yellow ones that hung above the streets. I tried to concentrate on a faraway landmark, an old technique I'd learned to avoid getting carsick, but I kept misjudging distances and my landmarks slipped past the sides of the car. He got on 59 headed south. I studied his profile, watched his mouth moving.

"Where are we going?" I said.

"My place."

That sounded good, to be at a place. If I could lie down on a cold floor and stop moving I'd be all right.

"Is there a floor?" I said.

"A floor in my apartment? Of course there's a floor."

"What's it like?"

"It has carpet. And there's tile in the kitchen and the bathroom."

"Okay," I said.

We passed the Denny's sign and the Hooters sign. A car to the right of us honked its horn and Peter swerved left. He must be fucked up, too. We passed under the Loop, and gloom closed around me. We were practically halfway to Sugar Land. Far from home. I rolled my window down for air, to help me think more clearly. I stretched my arm out the window, let my hand ride the current of wind. It didn't look like a hand, it looked like an animal. It wasn't until they were right behind us that I saw the red and blue lights flash in the mirror.

"Peter, pull over," I said.

"I am! What the fuck. Fuck," he said. "This is your fucking fault."

This sounded unlikely to me, so I ignored it. He parked on the shoulder.

"You're the one distracting me," he said. "Talking about my fucking carpet while I'm trying to fucking drive. Get me the insurance card. In the glove compartment."

I reached for it, and the cop on his loudspeaker yelled, "Hands on the dash."

We waited in the car. Peter was freaking out in the seat beside me.

"Fuck, fuck, fuck," he kept saying.

I examined my hands. Bits of chipped polish remained in the center of each nail. Maybe tomorrow I could get a manicure. Fake nails like Danielle's.

"This is exactly what I don't need," Peter said. Like a grouchy kid.

"He's coming," I said.

"Eliza—" he said.

"My name's not Eliza," I said.

"License and proof of insurance," the cop said.

The cop, a Latino guy with a big belly, examined Peter's documents and shined his light in Peter's face, then mine.

"Do you know why I stopped you, sir?" he said.

"Uh. Speeding?" Peter said.

"Step out of the car, sir."

Peter had some trouble with his seat belt. The cop made him kneel behind the car with his hands on his head. I hadn't been stopped by the police since I was about seventeen, ran a red light, I think, and the guy let me off without a ticket. Unlike Peter, I was an excellent drunk driver, having had a lot of practice. I strained to listen through the waves of traffic. Peter argued. He stood up and the cop watched him try to touch his nose with his finger. I sat there and sat there. Another squad car stopped behind the first one. Peter yelled, the cop yelled, and the cop cuffed him and shoved him in the backseat of the cruiser. The two cops stood around talking to each other.

I hoped one of these guys would give me a ride home. After a while I wondered if they'd forgotten about me, then I thought how silly, of course they hadn't, then I wondered again. My head was filling with gravel. A big truck charged past and blew a cloud of dirt and exhaust into the car. Exhaust, my fellow inhabitant. We lived together in Peter's car.

The rhythm of pain in my head matched itself to the beat of traffic. Normally I loved the sound of cars on the freeway; it oriented me, comforted me. I'd gone to sleep to the sound every night of my life. Now the wind rattled the gravel in my head, knocking the pieces against each other. Each stone had its own headache. I reached over to the ignition and turned the key so I could raise the windows against the noise. I was thirsty.

The speaker blasted inside my head. "Hands on the dash. Don't move."

I began to imagine the many possible ways I might have

avoided my current situation. I could've told Peter I had gon-
orrhea, for instance. Or I could've called a cab. I'd be home, I
could pour a glass of cold water and count out some aspirins. I
could be in the bath, I could be in bed. I wondered how late it
was. Shit, maybe I could even be at the bar.

The gravel inside me mutated into pulsating living animals. They were eating my internal organs and spitting them
out and eating them again. I sweated and bristled where anything touched me—the seat of the car, my clothing, the air. I
pushed the car door open and fell to the ground on my hands
and knees, retching and gagging.

"Fucking fuck, man," one cop said to the other.

I stood and leaned against Peter's car, picking pieces of
gravel out of my knees. My head still pounded steadily, but at
least the animals in my body held still. I spat bile. I faced the
cops, squinted to hear them.

"You take her, man."

"Fuck."

"I had mine done yesterday. Fresh pine scent."

"Fuck."

"'Sides, I got the dumbass already."

"Fuck, man."

"Plus I was here first."

"Yeah, yeah, yeah." The second one glanced at me. "All
right, lady."

"Please," I said. "Can you take me home?"

"Sure, honey, tell me where you wanna go." He snorted and
the other one shook his head, a weary acknowledgment.

"Come on, I didn't—"

"Public intox."

"What?"

"Soon as you got out of the car. Public."

"Sir, I'm sorry, I didn't mean—"

"Public intox and resisting an officer. You barf in my car, I'll charge you with property damage, too." He looked me over carefully. "You gonna barf again?"

"I don't think so," I said.

A wrecker parked in front of Peter's car. A guy got out and came towards us. I held my phone in my hand. Who could I call? I scrolled through my contacts. Nobody. I thought of the business card, Detective Ash's card. I dialed and left him a message.

The second cop came over and cuffed my wrists behind me. He led me by the arm. His grip crushed me.

"Ow," I said.

"All right, honey. Settle down."

He pushed me into the backseat, encased in hard plastic like a prefab shower stall. Easy to clean, I guess, but no one had lately. The car smelled sour from leftover sweat and vomit. I had to sit sideways to accommodate my cuffed hands. My officer muttered into his radio and joined the other two men by Peter's car. After a while he got in and nosed the cruiser into traffic. We headed west, towards the edges of the city. It became clear that someone, at some point during the night, had made a bad decision. I felt glad to be so wasted. If I'd been sober, I was sure I would be panicking.

After a few miles and many bursts of staticky speech on the radio, the cop stopped the car in a bright lot, got out, and opened my door. With the same grip on my arm he hauled me through the entrance to a squat building.

"Please," I said. "I'm innocent."

My head was killing me now. He pushed me down a hall of painted cinder block, the ceiling lined with fluorescent lights. Their buzzing got inside me and pried at the front of my skull, splintering it apart. We went into a room that contained two cells filled with women. Sweat and perfume replaced the air. The noise fluctuated enough so you couldn't get used to it, couldn't tune it out. He uncuffed me.

"I'm putting her in Two," my officer yelled behind him.

I needed to lie down. Bad. I had to get away from those lights. He unlocked a door to the cell and pushed me in. The room was cold, too air-conditioned. I felt not the least bit drunk anymore.

I glanced at the other women inside—there were seven or eight of them—and cast my eyes down immediately. One woman's teeth chattered. I could hear it from where I stood. She rubbed her arms and stamped her feet, crazed and exhausted, probably coming down off crack. I marveled at the force of her suffering. She had one whole corner of the cell to herself. A couple of others, young girls, kept their eyes on the floor. Two Latinas stood together whispering. They glared at me.

I stayed at the front of the cell, staring into the hall. The steel wall smelled like the metal risers we sat on in grade-school music class, hitting our triangles. A different cop came and retrieved one of the quiet girls. The crackhead began a high undulating keen, like rabbits dying, which I'd heard once, on a science class field trip in ninth grade. We were supposed to be cataloging the plants in a square meter of this meadow, and some stray dog discovered a nest nearby and killed the baby bunnies. Jail kept reminding me of school. The crackhead's dark skin looked gray. She smelled like she'd shit herself. Each of us shrank farther into our respective corners.

An aerosol scent hovered around the whispering girls, who were edging towards me. I wished I had a cigarette. I breathed in a cloud of hair spray and coughed.

"I don't think so," the girl said. "You did not just cough your nasty up in here."

"Sorry," I said, keeping my eyes down.

"This white bitch say sorry," the girl said to her friend.

They snickered. One of them came closer, stood right behind me.

"I like your hair," she said into my ear. I tried not to recoil.

"Hey!" she shrieked. "I'm talking to you!"

"Sorry," I said. "Thanks."

The other one edged behind me now. She had a blurred tattoo on her cheek that I couldn't make out; I didn't look directly at it. Her eyebrows were plucked and scabbed over and covered in pencil.

"You not being rude to my girl," this eyebrow person said. "Are you?"

"No," I said. "Sorry."

"She say she like your hair."

"Sorry," I said again.

I yelped at a sudden sharp sting on my scalp. The girls cackled. The one with the eyebrows held a few strands of my hair.

"What the fuck?" I said.

She twisted my hair in her fists like she could strangle me with it and took a sudden step forward. I jumped back, banging my head on the wall. The girls snickered and reclaimed their corner, whispering to each other. Every few minutes one would say, "What the fuck!" in a whiny white girl voice—it sounded exactly like me. The other one would say "Sorry," and double over in laughter. I gazed resolutely out through the bars, flinching at every noise behind me.

"Ford," a lady cop said. She unlocked the barred door. "Come on."

She motioned down the hall and closed the cell behind us, but I could still hear the crackhead's muted wail. We stopped at a desk and the cop gave me my purse, sweater, driver's license.

I signed for them and walked into the lobby. Detective Ash leaned against a desk.

"You're here," I said. "You came."

His hand pressed the small of my back and propelled me out the door. I had to close my eyes against the bright lights in the parking lot.

"Jesus," he said. "I can smell the whiskey."

"Thank you," I said. "I mean, for coming. Thank you, you have no idea how much this means to me, in there, it was horrible—" I started to cry.

"You're welcome," he said. "Did they process you? Get your prints?"

"No," I said.

"Good, that's good."

We headed north. The downtown skyline clumped on the horizon. I relaxed in the seat and rubbed my head where I'd banged it. He exited before my street and parked in front of House of Pies.

"Breakfast?" he said.

"You really don't have to—"

"Why not. Let's get some pancakes."

"I used to come here a lot."

"Why'd you stop?" he said.

"I realized I hated it."

He laughed but I was serious. House of Pies is a shithole. We sat in a vinyl booth textured to resemble leather. The place had been done up in orange and brown and yellow—to simulate grease, perhaps. The rips in the upholstery were patched with plastic tape that peeled up and stuck to my legs. We ordered coffee and eggs and strawberry pie piled high with Cool Whip. They brought the pie first. A maraschino cherry leaked red rivulets in the topping. The eggs came. Suddenly I was starving.

When had I last eaten? I scarfed the food. Ash stretched his arms along the back of the booth.

"Better?" he asked.

I shrugged. I decided to never drink again.

"Not the greatest night of your life, is it?"

"I'm sorry about this," I said. "I've never been to jail before."

"I know," he said. "I checked."

"Oh."

His lips turned up slightly at the corners. His shirt was open to the second button, sleeves cuffed to the middle of his forearms. Neon from the window lit his face. Even in this oily light he looked handsome, in control.

"Why did you come?" I asked. "I didn't think you would."

"Why did you call?"

I smashed the pie with my fork, didn't answer. He must have figured it out already—there wasn't anyone else.

After a minute he said, "I owe you an apology."

"You?" I said. "What for?"

"I shouldn't have shown you those photographs," he said. "I didn't know you'd react like that."

"It's okay," I said.

"How's your head?"

"Fine." The cut scabbed at my hairline, but my bangs covered it and you could hardly tell.

"I'm glad," he said. "I wondered if I should have taken you to the hospital."

"No need," I said.

"Good. So. How well did you know him?"

"Who?"

"The driver of the car. Peter Randall Sones. DUI, marijuana possession, resisting arrest."

"Is it worse if I knew him well or I didn't know him?"

"You tell me, Charlotte. He's your boyfriend."

"He's not my boyfriend. I met him tonight. It was a mistake."

Ash nodded.

"I don't have a boyfriend," I said.

"You miss her?" he said.

"What? Who?"

"Danielle Reeves."

"Please," I said. "Do we have to talk about that right now?"

He shrugged. The waitress trundled over and filled our stained mugs. Ash's eyes were a rich blue, full of kindness. Until him, I had never seen anyone look attractive in House of Pies. I moved my gaze to the dark parking lot, but I saw only our reflection in the window. My blouse was wrinkled and dirty.

"It's just, I was thinking," he said. "You told me everything Danielle said that day you met. Right?"

"Yeah," I said.

"Even the tiniest details could be important. You might know something that you don't even know you know. You have to tell me every little thing you can think of."

"I did," I said.

"Good. I just wondered if you thought of anything else."

"So you don't have any leads, then?"

"We're still in the information-gathering stage. We are talking to everyone she saw those last couple of days. Everyone she saw on a regular basis."

"And?"

"And I don't know. There's some unusual things. Things that were not part of her routine."

"Like what?"

"Like you, Charlotte."

"I didn't do anything," I said.

"I'm not accusing you. I'm just noticing what changed in

Danielle's life, what was different. She saw you for the first time in years, right? It's unusual. Anything outside of the regular pattern, I have to pay close attention to."

"You think me seeing Danielle—you think I caused it?"

"I don't know," he said. "Maybe not intentionally. What do you think?"

"Jesus," I said. I felt more tired than I'd been in my whole life. "I can't deal with this right now."

He looked at me over the Formica table. Studied me for a moment, then nodded.

"Okay," he said. "Let's get you home."

He slid out of the booth. I unpeeled the tape from my thighs and stood. I fell asleep on the ten-minute drive to my place and woke with him leaning over me, unbuckling my seat belt.

"Come on, Charlotte, you're home," he said.

I leaned into him as he walked me up the stairs. My head fit nicely under the curve of his collarbone. I searched for the key.

"Charlotte," he said, "don't forget to lock the door."

"Okay."

He waited for me to go in.

"Detective?" I said.

"Yeah."

"You're nice to me."

"Yeah," he said. "Go get some sleep."

I lay on the bed while the sun came up. Before I fell asleep I remembered this lamp we'd had, me and my mom. The base was thick frosted glass with a mountain scene painted on the inside. You could put a separate bulb inside the base to make the picture glow. I used to study that glowing landscape and imagine us there in the mountains, inside the lamp, and she would be healthy and strong, no one would be mad at us, and we would be together.

Things weren't always easy with my mom. She had been ill as long as I could remember, and the doctors never knew what was wrong. She mostly sat in her special chair, watching television or staring out the window, oblivious to her surroundings. That was fine. I took care of us. But when her pain went into remission she quit taking her pills. I would come home from school to a dark TV and an empty chair, and music playing. The apartment had an awake feeling and the sharp smell of cleaning products. She would call out from the other room, where she was scrubbing the bathroom or dusting her shelves full of knickknacks. She would say she was quitting the medicine, that she didn't need it anymore, and now she'd be a real mom and get a job, and we would eat at restaurants. I always tried to believe her. She looked so pretty and alive.

My mother hated the drugs, but she didn't know how to be sober. How could she? She'd never had a chance to learn. Without the meds, she'd go into withdrawal, and try to handle it with gin. She was a bad drunk, chaotic, angry. Her moods shifted drastically. Sometimes I would find her seething, pacing our apartment, pulling dishes off the shelves and shattering them. She often ended up cut and bloody.

One day the lamp disappeared. I came home from school and it was gone. I assumed it got broken. I knew better than to ask her. She was back on the meds, docile and clearly in pain. There was no point. It would only make her feel bad.

Outside, dawn lit the smog. I lay in bed, closed my eyes, and pictured the mountain scene, its purple frosted light and tiny cedars dusted with white. I drifted off among the trees.

CHAPTER SIX

I woke in the late afternoon, fuzzy and unsettled. I couldn't
remember much of the night before. I checked my purse and
my pockets for clues. My cigarettes were gone. I'd either lost
them or smoked them. I checked my phone and saw a voice mail
from Sally, plus the café had called four times. I had completely
missed my shift. My manager would be gone by now. I'd have to
go in and talk to him. I hoped I wasn't fired.

I listened to the message from Sally. I'd never heard her
voice shake like this.

"Charlotte, honey, it's Sally Reeves. I guess you heard what
happened. If you're free this evening could you stop over? We
need to talk. It's important."

I didn't want to see Sally ever again. But what could I do?
Her daughter was dead. I showered and dressed, still feeling
like shit. I went outside and discovered my car wasn't there.
Okay, I must've left it at the bar. I rode my bike to the corner
store for cigarettes and smoked one on my way to the Harp. My
old Nissan sat alone under the magnolia at the rear of the lot.

I angled the bike into the trunk and drove to the Vietnamese deli on Travis for coffee and a banh mi.

Cars on Milam Street whirled light through the plate-glass window. I finished my sandwich, even the jalapenos, the heat of the peppers waking me. I smoked and flipped through the paper. Danielle's murder was on the front page and in the Metro section. They had printed a photograph of the motel where Danielle died, an old, shabby place. I wondered why she had gone there. Another photo of an interior had the caption, "A room in the Astro Motel similar to the one where Reeves' body was found." It didn't look particularly special—a bed, a lamp, a mirror, a sink. No blood anywhere, no indication of the gore in those other photographs, the ones the detective showed me.

I turned to the inside of the Metro section and saw an old picture of Danielle that I remembered from high school. She wore my shirt in the photo, a thrift-store T-shirt with a silk-screened swing set on the front. She stretched it out—her boobs were bigger than mine, even before she got them done—so I had let her keep it. Next to that was a family photo I hadn't seen before, taken when Danielle was about twelve and already pretty in a sultry, grown-up way.

I left the paper on the table and stopped on Fannin to buy flowers, a white bouquet of lilies and some tiny round buds, I forgot their name. I spent a lot. It was Sally's money, after all. I wondered if Danielle would have liked them. If she even liked flowers. We never bought flowers, or talked about flowers. Flowers weren't exactly a part of our lives.

I took Montrose to West Gray and made my way to Sally's. The house rose behind a giant lawn with a walk that led straight from the curb to the front door. Before Danielle, I'd never met anybody who lived in River Oaks. Their house was a medium-sized mansion with a gray stone façade. As a kid I was dazzled by it. The rooms appeared to multiply, another and then another; I couldn't retain the whole floor plan in my mind at once. A housekeeper came every day and kept the kitchen stocked with artisan breads, nice cheeses, and olives. The fridge always contained fancy leftovers from some catered party— duck quesadillas, wilted kale, smoked salmon. I wore Danielle's clothes, which the housekeeper washed and hung in the closet. I loved the food and how clean everything was. The art on the walls cost a fortune.

Now Sally answered my knock in stocking feet, no jacket, her blouse tucked into her suit skirt.

"Thanks for stopping by, sweetie," she said. "Come on in."

The house looked the same as I remembered it: huge and clean, a little sterile. And way too big for one person. How did Sally feel, moving around in her expensive house, alone? I handed her the bouquet.

"Oh, they're lovely, Charlotte," she said. "I'll get a vase. Can I offer you a drink? I'm having wine."

"Sure," I said. I could use it.

"Sit down."

She gestured into the adjacent parlor, furnished with antiques and a woven rug that matched the drapes. Danielle and I had never spent time in this room. We hung out by the pool, mostly, and upstairs. Sally returned with the wine bottle and handed me a glass. She sat opposite me in a wing chair, the coffee table between us. Her toenails were painted a red that showed through her stockings. For some reason the toes bothered me. It was too intimate, seeing her without shoes, like she was half naked.

"I'm sorry for your loss," I said, and grimaced at the cliché.

"Well, you lost her, too," Sally said. "It's a difficult time."

"Yes," I said.

I wanted to gulp my wine but I wasn't sure she'd refill it. I sipped it, replacing my glass on the coaster.

"I'm glad you came," she said. "There are a couple of issues we need to discuss."

I wondered if she wanted the money back. I didn't have it all; I'd spent a lot on drinks.

"Charlotte," she said, "how did this happen?"

"I have no idea."

"You must know something. Who did this, Charlotte? Who did this to her? She's dead now, you can tell me."

"Why are you asking me?"

"You girls always kept secrets from me. I'm not an idiot. She must have brought this on herself."

I gaped at her, heard the disgust in her tone. She hated Danielle, even dead. She always had.

"I deserve to know the truth," she said. "I'm her mother."

"No," I said, louder than I meant to. "I don't know what happened, I wasn't involved."

She glared at me and I looked back, unblinking. I imagined her business rivals crumbling under that gaze. She was nothing but a bully.

"I need a cigarette," I said.

I stood and carried my wine towards the door. I closed it behind me and stood under the enormous lantern to smoke. In a minute Sally came out, carrying the bottle.

"Charlotte, forgive me," she said. "That wasn't fair. I can't believe she's gone."

She looked broken now, confused. I wished I hadn't raised my voice.

"I can't believe it either," I said.

"Let's go around the side," she said. "There's the outdoor living room. It's new, I don't think you've seen it."

We walked through an iron gate to a courtyard she'd had built, a copper fire pit surrounded by cushioned wicker couches. I lit another cigarette.

"Would you mind?" she said, gesturing towards the pack.

"You smoke?" I said.

"Not normally."

She lit the cigarette and took a few inexpert puffs. She held it carefully. Her feet were still in stockings and I kept thinking the tiles would snag them and make a run. Holding a cigarette, her hands reminded me of Danielle's. I thought, Danielle is gone and Sally is the ghost.

"I needed you here because I have a favor to ask," she said. She sounded so vulnerable, struggling for composure. I felt guilty now.

"What can I do?"

"Are you aware that this matter is getting a lot of media attention?"

"I saw the paper today," I said, thinking, *This matter?* Is that what we were calling it?

"There are elements that Danielle would have preferred to be kept private. It's important that we respect her memory. You more than anyone can understand that."

"Elements? What do you mean?"

"Oh, come on, Charlotte. What she did for a living. Lord knows what else she was involved in. Imagine that splashing all over CNN."

"Oh," I said.

"I would appreciate it if you didn't talk to any reporters."

"I see."

"I'm glad you understand."

"Did the cops tell you?" I said.

"Tell me what?" she said.

"That Danielle made porn."

"I'd rather not talk about that," she said. "I don't think Danielle would want us to."

"She never was good enough for you," I said, angry. "You never cared how she felt or what she wanted, only how things looked."

Sally paled. Amazed, I watched the color sink from her face. I'd scared her. How often did anyone scare her? It made me feel reckless and powerful.

"Charlotte, please. You have to understand. She's dead. My daughter. I'm asking you this favor."

"Yeah," I said. "I know she's dead. You don't have to keep saying it."

"Think of all I've done for you," she said. "I took care of you, all those years."

"And now you're cashing in," I said.

"Charlotte, I don't mean it like that. Please. I'm sorry, I'm not myself."

She was bad at begging, bad at needing help from other people. I could tell she hadn't had to do it much in her life. She struggled to keep the frustration out of her words. Her phone rang from inside the house, and she tossed her cigarette in the fire pit.

She looked tired and old, and I felt sorry for her, disgusted at my cruelty. I hated how Sally always tried to spin everything, always tried to manage Danielle. Still, I remembered Danielle's embarrassment about the porn, her reluctance about telling me. She hadn't even wanted *me* to know. Sally went in to get the phone and the outdoor lights came on—lanterns along the path, a garland of golden bulbs strung on the trellis to my left. It was getting dark.

I had a flash of memory from the night before, of Ash bending over me in the car. Suddenly the whole night resurfaced—the holding cell, that woman screaming in the corner, the girl who pulled my hair. I felt sickened, and sickening, like I was a poison I couldn't stop swallowing. Paralyzed by shame, I stared at the floral pattern on the cushions until my focus went soft. I gulped my wine, lit a new cigarette, and sucked the smoke deep inside. I wanted anything that came from outside myself. Any foreign substance.

Ash. I had never let another person see me that pathetic. Not since middle school, anyhow, when everybody knew my mom took drugs and my clothes were always wrinkled. Fury at myself brought on a sudden vertigo, a starting and stopping, as in a dream of falling. I imagined myself in a car crash, a violent death, going over a cliff. Through a barrier and into empty air, to shatter on the rocks below. Not that there were any cliffs in Houston. This place was so flat you could see the curve of the earth.

I looked at my hands in my lap. With my nails I pinched the webbed skin between my thumb and forefinger. A tiny crescent of blood grew. I licked it. The skin on my hands had always been thin, fragile. Like my mom's. She complained about it. If she was feeling okay, she was diligent about moisturizing. She kept tubs of cocoa butter in the kitchen, the bathroom, by the bed and the TV. When the pain increased she took the Oxy and it knocked her out for days in a row—sometimes weeks. Her hands would get scratchy and dry. She lay there and gazed at the ceiling until it was time for her pills. The smell of cocoa butter always made me miss her. Made me nervous.

Sally appeared, the phone in her hand. She had slipped on a pair of ballet flats. I stood.

"You don't have to worry," I said. "I'm not going to talk to reporters. I wasn't going to anyways."

"Oh, Charlotte, I can't tell you how relieved I am," she said. "Thank you."

I shrugged.

She said, "The memorial service is tomorrow. You should be there. Will you come?"

"I guess so," I said.

"Good. It's at the Episcopal church on Alabama. Three o'clock."

"Okay."

"I'm glad. Lord have mercy if her other friends show up. I can't imagine what they'll be wearing."

"What they'll be wearing?" I said. "You're afraid the other porn stars will embarrass you."

Her face crumpled and she made an involuntary sound, the beginning of a sob. I watched her regain control, and she stared at me, smooth and full of rage.

"I don't deserve this," she said. "Not any of it." Her voice was icy.

"Neither did she," I said.

We watched one another for a long moment. Her hands shook, I noticed. I was shaking, too. Finally she turned away, to face the pool and the privacy fence beyond.

"I'm going," I said to her rigid back.

"Wait," she said, turning. "One more thing, please."

"What?"

"I know you saw her, you spoke to her."

"Yes."

"Did she say anything about me?"

"Not really," I said.

"What does that mean, not really?"

"She asked what you wanted," I said. "That's pretty much it."

I could have told her about Danielle refusing the money, but I didn't want to get into it. I walked around the house and let

myself in to get my purse. I drove and got lost in the curvy River
Oaks streets, then headed west on Memorial, past the park and
the Loop, through subdivisions. I kept driving, hoping to dis-
lodge the film of sorrow and anger that clung to me, clutched at
my heels, my hair. Hoping to get away from the difficult world.
I drove until I didn't feel anything anymore. I drove and drove,
the radio silent, the windows open to the soft wet air.

The air had a sound as I moved my car through it. I listened
and thought of physics, the behavior of sound in outer space.
It must be different, faster or quieter, maybe. If sound had no
atmosphere to travel through, did it arrive more quickly or did
it simply die? Maybe the emptiness trapped it so it couldn't go
anywhere, forever stuck at its source. I couldn't remember how
it worked, though I'd surely learned it in school. The question
was like a koan, except that it was science; I had simply forgotten the answer.

This one night—it was maybe junior year—Danielle and I
took some pills, I don't remember what, and cruised around. I'm
surprised we didn't wreck. We were on the east side, near the
ship channel, a part of town I never went to. Danielle turned on
a side street near a big refinery and we parked facing it, watching the flames atop the towers. It looked like a miniature city,
futuristic and menacing. Its smoke lit white in the sky before
fading into general smog.

"It's cool, isn't it?" Danielle said. We walked over the weed-
cracked asphalt and tar seams still soft from the day. We
stretched out on the hood of her car, leaning against the windshield, smoking a joint. We'd left the radio on. Contaminants
laced the air.

"Too bad it smells so weird," I said.

"My uncle used to bring me out this way, to the Ninfa's on
Navigation. We'd get dinner the nights Sally worked late."

"I didn't know you had an uncle."

"Sally's brother. He moved to Colorado. I used to go to his house in the afternoons. He picked me up from school my sixth grade year, it was right after my dad left. They knew us there, at the restaurant. I always got the kids' meal. Fajitas and a queso puff."

"I love queso puffs," I said. "I could eat one right now." I was high.

"I think Sally paid him to take care of me. She was always at work. He didn't have a job."

She sounded strange, like her words came from far off.

"You keep in touch with him?" I said.

"He sends me a birthday card with twenty dollars in it every year. I always throw it out."

"Even the money?"

"Yeah. I don't need his fucking money."

"Shit, you should give it to me," I said. "I'd take it."

"Ha. Too late." Her birthday was a month ago already.

"You're a spoiled brat."

"Yep." She laughed.

"Why do you throw the money away?" I said.

"He used to fuck me."

"What?" I said.

She pointed at the refinery, the pipes interwoven, going every direction.

"I loved driving past here. You can see it from the freeway. I used to pretend fairies lived in it. They made the fires with their magic."

"Are you serious?" I said. "It's not funny."

"Give me a cigarette."

She wasn't smiling. We sat smoking, listening to the car radio. I was shocked.

"Does Sally know?" I said.

"I told her, after he moved away," she said. "It's weird, though. I don't think she remembers."

"How could she not?"

"It was a long time ago. There was a lot going on."

"Danielle, that doesn't make sense."

"She was such a freak after my dad left. It would have upset her and caused problems. She didn't want me home alone. Without Uncle Alex I would have to take the bus home from school and be by myself in the afternoons."

"But maybe if you'd told her sooner—"

"She wouldn't have cared, she was fucked up already. The divorce was bad. My parents were both such jerks. She worked late, she got drunk every night on her fancy bottles of wine. I basically stayed in my room and watched TV."

"Danielle, my god. I'm sorry."

"Why are you apologizing? It should be her. She should apologize."

"Well, he should," I said. "Fucking bastard."

"He came to visit, at Thanksgiving. I guess it was a couple of years later. We had a bunch of people at our house. And he showed up."

"What happened?" I asked.

"Nothing. He ate dinner. I didn't talk to him, I was at the kids' table in the breakfast room. They gave us that sparkling apple juice that comes in a fake champagne bottle."

"Why didn't she throw him out? Or call the police?"

"I don't know. I figured she must have forgotten. How could she invite him to Thanksgiving?"

She was crying then. I hugged her.

"God, I hate her," Danielle said. "I fucking hate her."

Later, after she started dancing, she talked about the abuse openly, like it wasn't a big deal. She mentioned details, coloring books he'd bought her. He used to close the curtains and make her undress in the middle of the living room. He liked to sit in this big recliner while she watched TV naked. She liked this show, an after-school soap opera for kids called *Tribes*. I remembered it; I'd watched it, too. Danielle said a lot of the dancers at the club had been molested. She joked about it being a prerequisite for the job, that they might as well ask about it in the audition. The recliner, she said, was blue.

It was all such a long time ago. As I drove I thought, No one cares about that now.

I kept driving, longing for a silent, dark place, beyond the streetlights and the lights of the city. But the city never stopped, it reached and reached. There was no sky beyond the hovering, staining smog. I killed my headlights, as a test, and I could see the road easily, lit by the air. The grid stretched endlessly, inescapable. I made a U-turn on the wide road, headed to the center of town, wishing there was somebody who could help me, tell me what to do.

CHAPTER SEVEN

I slept terribly and woke too early, with echoes of Danielle's voice in my head. I couldn't believe she was gone, right when we were going to be friends again. I was pissed at Sally, too, for all the ways she hurt Danielle over the years. And then, two days after I put them in touch, Danielle wound up murdered. It had to be coincidence, but I felt uneasy. I wished I'd never gone to see Sally in the first place.

My thoughts turned to Michael. What right did he have to break up with me just when I needed him? I hated feeling this angry. To distract myself, I called work and asked for the manager, hoping he wouldn't be there.

I waited a few minutes, sipping coffee and listening to the hold music. Andrew came on the line.

"Charlotte," he said, "where were you yesterday?"

"I'm sorry, Andrew. I know I screwed up. This has been the worst week of my life. Please don't fire me."

"Charlotte, it was two days in a row. First you're late, then you don't show up at all, no phone call, nothing. I had to come in on my day off."

"I'm so sorry, really. Look, my friend was killed on Tuesday."

I didn't mention Michael dumping me, or going to jail. I told him about the murder, and about Detective Ash, and that I'd been held by the police the whole night before I missed my shift. He listened. I think he believed me.

"I've already made the schedule for next week," he said. "You're not on it."

"I understand."

"Charlotte, take the week and get yourself together, okay?"

"Okay. I have to go to the funeral, anyway."

"Come in and talk to me if you want back on the schedule."

"Thank you," I said.

"I mean it. Take care of yourself," he said, and hung up.

The kindness in his voice made me start to cry. I paced from window to window, surveying the street, the side yard, the dusty vase on the neighbor's windowsill. I trimmed some unraveling strings on the rug. I wished I could talk to someone about going to Sally's last night. There was no one I could call. I hated Michael for not being there. For leaving me alone. Even if we were still together it would have been too much to explain. Nobody besides Danielle would understand.

I poured whiskey into my coffee mug and flipped through some old pictures of Danielle. I found one taken in my apartment right after graduation. Pot smoke mingled with the light coming through the living room windows, obscuring her hair, making it even more blond. The cloud of light touched her down one side as she smiled at the camera, her heavy-lidded eyes blinking at the smoke. I wished I'd taken more photos, gotten in touch with her sooner, seen her more. It seemed impossible that she was gone.

On my laptop I opened Danielle's website and paid the eighteen dollars with my debit card. I wanted to see her, that was all. I watched a video of Audrey and Danielle together in a room with dark walls. Danielle wore garters and black stilettos, her blond waves held with a shell clip. She stood and spoke, and I muted the volume—her voice was more than I could stand.

Audrey's body draped along a red upholstered bench. She wore a simple loose dress of some nearly transparent fabric. Her feet were bare, her toenails unpolished. Danielle bent at the waist to kiss her, displaying her ass for the camera. She pushed Audrey's dress up her tan thigh. The next shot showed Audrey kissing Danielle's tits, Audrey's hands everywhere on her. Danielle closed her eyes in a simulation of pleasure. Their bodies writhed and panted.

The camera zoomed out to show them on the bench, moving together, groping one another, and cut to the doorway where a man stood. He was shirtless, muscled. He pulled Danielle by the arm, attached her mouth to his cock, which she sucked automatically. Another guy came in, yanked Audrey's dress over her head and tossed it aside. I lit a cigarette and fast-forwarded to a close-up of Danielle. She pulled a lock of hair behind her ear. The lines of her fingers, the grace of her movement—I'd seen her perform that same gesture, thoughtlessly, a million times. I rewound the video and watched again as she tucked her hair behind her ear. She died and left this, of all things.

I didn't want to go to the memorial service, but I knew I had to. I wished Michael were with me. I had to figure out what to wear. To my mom's funeral I'd worn a dress I'd borrowed from Danielle. My closet contained a bunch of crappy work clothes and sundresses, nothing appropriate. I finished my drink and went shopping.

I tried the vintage stores on Westheimer, a row of brightly colored old bungalows with piles of dusty clothes crammed in every room. In the first shop a limping orange cat chased me into the dressing room. It sprawled on the floor and batted at the dressing room curtain, blue polyester that clung to its fur. I needed to look subdued, respectable. I had no idea how. I tried on a few dresses, but they weren't right. The place gave me allergies.

I navigated lunchtime traffic to the Village, full of high-fashion boutiques and trendy local designers. My favorite, Imperial Palace, was housed in an old Chinese buffet restaurant. Mannequins in the windows sat at lacquered tables, chopsticks tied with ribbons to their hands, or they stood holding trays of fake egg rolls. One wore a garland of fortune cookies strung together with a length of yarn. The store still smelled greasy.

A guy wearing a women's military-style blouse with lace epaulets asked if he could help.

"I need a dress for a funeral," I said.

"Ooh," he said. "Sorry."

I held a blue jersey dress with appliquéd butterflies at the hem. "What do you think of this one?"

"Maybe. Let's see what else we have."

"It's in an hour."

"Goddamn, girl!" he said. "A challenge. Tell you what. We have that one in black with black butterflies, let me go get it."

He raced to the stockroom, the old kitchen. I collected every black and blue and gray item in the shop. The clerk returned with piles of layered viscose, chiffon, and vintage lace. He showed me a red gown with a Chinese collar, sheer with a floral print underlay covering the torso.

"I like that one," I said. "Is it an old Hawaiian shirt?"

"Yeah," he said. "Thank you. It's mine."

"You designed this?"

He nodded, beaming. "I'm Luis."

"Charlotte," I said and we shook hands.

"The Chinese wear red for mourning," he said.

"I don't think that will work. This is a white girl."

I picked out one dress, black with a pink printed belt that tied around the waist. I stepped out of the dressing room.

"Oh, shit," he said. "Not everybody can pull that off. It's fantastic on you."

"Do you think people can tell it's guns on the sash?"

"No," he said. "No one will notice, it looks like an abstract pattern. And the pink isn't too much, either. People think you have to be conservative at a funeral, but that's not the case anymore."

"Really?" I said.

"You should take off your bra, though. It's showing here."

I did, and he tugged on the bustline of the dress.

"See, it's supposed to fit this way. There. Oh my god, I love it. Let's cut the tags off."

At the counter he bagged my other clothes and I paid. I was late. I sped over to the church and had to park in the unpaved part of the lot they reserved for Easter and Christmas services. My heels sank into the ground. I hurried to the entrance, dodging between media vans and luxury SUVs.

The church was a long gray building striped with stained glass and flanked by a bed of pansies. The neatly mulched flowers seemed too flimsy, out of place, penned in by a monkey grass border. Everything was too loud, too hot and bright—the traffic whizzing by and the damp steaming gutters. What did any of this have to do with Danielle? I wished I could disappear. I already regretted the stupid dress.

Arctic air-conditioning flooded the hall. The floors and walls, even the air, seemed polished to a sheen. Three sets of windowed double doors led into the chapel or the sanctuary, whatever you called it. I took a seat near the exit. People packed the place. They had decent clothes, refined bearing— Sally's friends. They weren't anybody Danielle would hang around with.

The minister lady read prayers and went on for a while about Jesus. Her voice sounded flushed, excited. The whole place felt wound up. Men tapped their knuckles, fidgeting. Women adjusted their clothes, patted their hair. It was because of the murder, and Danielle's youth, her beauty. They were delighted to be there, to be sad and outraged, a little afraid. To wonder who did it. To be part of it.

I couldn't shake the sense that this funeral, the murder, the cops, it was all some practical joke, that Danielle would walk in at any moment, laughing at us for being so serious.

For some reason I kept thinking of the difficult times with her. Once I'd slept at her house on a school night and we were smoking a joint by the pool. She was in a bad mood, mad at Sally, probably, and taking it out on me. I'd been reading García Márquez, and I read a line aloud to Danielle. Halfway through I could tell she thought it was lame. I finished the sentence anyway, and she said, "Yeah, that's *really* interesting." Sarcastic. She stubbed out the joint and dropped it in her pocket. "There's a Marilyn Monroe movie on cable."

She always decided what was cool and what was not. To me it seemed arbitrary. I tried to keep up, but I was always missing some important, supposedly obvious detail. Why did we like Marilyn Monroe movies and not *One Hundred Years of Solitude*? I had no idea. What could I do except follow her. She grinned at me and poured us drinks from Sally's liquor cabinet. We sat on opposite ends of the couch, stretched under a blanket in the air-conditioning, and she took my foot in her lap, absently, staring at the screen. I nearly cried in gratitude for the smile, the touch. I watched the movie and pretended I was fine. I laughed when she did. She had so much power over me. I used to get scared by how much I loved her and needed her.

The congregation stood for a hymn and I snuck out the door. I was freezing. I stepped into the hot afternoon. Reporters and camera people lined the steps. They glanced at me and away. I stood on the sidewalk and smoked.

Soon the church doors opened and the men and women in their somber clothes came down the steps, past the flower garden. The group of news people mobilized, jostling and craning their microphones. Sally emerged in a trim olive and cream suit. She looked flushed, younger. She accepted the hands of her friends, nodded, leaned in for air kisses.

The reporters flocked around her. She patted her hair and turned to the cameras, a mournful and brave expression mounted on her face. She wore the same glinty eyes I had seen in the framed photographs at her office, of her with George Bush, with the mayor and the Rockets coach.

Detective Ash stood off to the side of the reporters. He wore a gray suit. Mourners filed past him to their cars. He saw me walking over and nodded, continued scanning the crowd.

"Hi," I said.

"Charlotte," he said. "Nice dress."

"Thank you," I said, not sure if he was making fun of me.

"Listen," he said. "About the other night. I don't want to get a call like that again. You need to take better care of yourself."

I didn't know how to respond. His attention fastened to someone near the throng by the side entrance. All the energy in the air surged into his body.

"Excuse me," he said over his shoulder, already weaving between cars and people. He stopped near a group of guys and singled one out, a curly-haired man, slightly built. I couldn't hear what they were saying. The guy looked tense and twitchy. He kept glancing towards his friends.

I walked next door to the West Alabama Ice House. Regulars, bikers and neighborhood people, crowded the picnic benches, along with other funeral goers. The bartender reached into the deep cooler in front of him and pulled bottles from the slushy ice. I ordered a beer.

"You get a lot of overflow from the church?" I asked him.

"Weddings and funerals. We have to bring in an extra fridge. The wiring's a nightmare."

He pointed to an orange extension cord that ran from the refrigerator across the pavement and up the trunk of a Mexican birch, where it connected with another extension cord. I lit a cigarette and drank half my beer in one long sip. Dust covered the afternoon. I perched on the end of a picnic table, checking first for splinters that could snag my new dress.

I spotted Audrey and waved. She came over with her beer and hugged me.

"Is that guns on your dress?" she said to me. "Don't you think that's in poor taste?"

"I thought it was subtle," I said, worried.

"Oh well, she wasn't shot."

People packed the yard as the afternoon wore on. Sally's entourage and the members of the press dispersed, their cars clearing the lot. Everyone else seemed to be drinking. The curly-haired man who'd been talking to Ash sat down with us.

"Hey," Audrey said to him. "Charlotte, meet Brandon Young."

"Hi," I said.

"I saw you at the church," he said. "How did you know Danielle?"

"Charlotte went to school with Dani," Audrey said.

"That was you," he said. "Her friend she went to meet."

"She told me about you," I said. "You make the movies, right?"

"Yeah."

"Audrey invited me to your screening. It sounded cool."

"I'm not doing it now," he said.

"Do you have any pot?" Audrey asked.

Brandon shrugged and I said no.

"Fuckin' shit," Audrey said. Her comment seemed to refer to a greater lack, an acknowledgment of our total unpreparedness for this situation.

"Fuckin' shit," I agreed. The three of us clinked beers and drank.

Audrey looked weary and despondent for a second, before taking up her smile again. The transition on her face, I'd seen it before, in her movies. I blushed.

"Who are these people?" she asked, nodding to a cluster of folks in expensive suits. Sally's colleagues, I guessed.

"Cops and robbers," I said, thinking about Ash.

Brandon had turned to talk to a couple of guys standing near us. They opened their circle and took us in, one of those smooth drunken happenings, like a microscopic video of mitosis in reverse. They wore black jeans and tucked-in shirts. Like me, these people had no idea how to dress for a funeral.

Audrey made introductions—Kenneth, Anthony, Brian, George. I recognized George from the porn site and felt embarrassed. He pulled a flask from his pocket and handed it around. Audrey passed it to me. Vodka. It tasted like air-conditioning, crisp and clean. I could drink it forever.

"Man, I hated it in there," Kenneth said, indicating the church.

"I guess it's not supposed to be fun," I said.

"Sure, but, fuck. When I think about Dani, that's not what

I want to think about. I thought it would be spiritual or something."

"Spiritual?" I said.

"Danielle and I talked about that stuff once," he said.

"What'd she say?"

"She thought organized religion was bad, like it was commercial, and took advantage of people and stuff."

"Right. The standard junior high philosophy," I said.

"What," he said. "Don't you think it's true?"

"Sure it's true. It's obvious. That's why children can figure it out. So what?"

"She said she believed in God, though," he said.

I tried and failed to think of a more annoying conversation. How could Danielle have been friends with this guy?

"Where's Sylvie and Cass?" George asked.

"I texted Sylvie," said Brian. "She's staying home. They're scared. I mean, it could be some stalker. They're talking about quitting, leaving town."

"I don't blame them," George said. "It could have been someone we know."

"They could be here," Anthony said.

Audrey's eyes jumped, and she moved closer to Brandon. He squeezed her to his side.

"I don't get it," George said. "I mean, who the fuck would kill Danielle? It's crazy."

"Yeah, I mean, Danielle?" Brian said.

"Seriously, dude," George said. "She was sweet. Remember when she first came on set? She was like, professional from the beginning."

"She was never one of those whiny bitches," Anthony said.

"She was always cheerful. And, like, enthusiastic, even if she had a bad day," George said.

"Yeah," Anthony said. "She was always happy to fuck me. Like she *wanted* to. Remember that anal scene? The lube spilled and her hands kept slipping."

A couple of them laughed, apparently having forgotten their concerns about the identity of Danielle's murderer. Maybe it was one of them.

"And plus," Anthony said, "she seriously, genuinely loved to fuck. She loved to suck cock."

"Yeah, dude," George said. They high-fived.

"What a fucking waste," Anthony said, shaking his head. He looked up, unfocused, and I saw he was wildly drunk. He threw his arms open, sloshing beer on the dirt. "Now who's left?" he yelled. "Who've we got now? Just a bunch of fucking cunts!"

He stopped abruptly when his gaze registered Audrey. She trembled beside me like a hunting dog.

"You fuckcock," she said, her voice hoarse and whispery, full of pain.

Quiet came on like a thing fallen from the sky, in which we could hear the classic rock station playing the Eagles, Audrey panting in anger, and our feet shuffling in the dirt, uncertain. Anthony raised his hands to ward her off.

"Audrey," Brian said. "Audrey, calm down. We're gonna miss her, is all. Right, guys? Nobody was close to her like you, we know that."

"Yeah," Anthony said. "None of us had to use a strap-on." He grabbed his crotch and the rest of them giggled anxiously.

Brandon moved in with a quick blow to Anthony's face. The thud of his fist echoed. Brandon hit him twice more before anyone had a chance to react. You could see the punches hurt; the last one knocked Anthony into the person behind him, a grizzled lady with a lot of cleavage showing. She said, "Careful, darlin'," in a smoker's rumble. Her man shoved Anthony and shouted. In an instant three of his buddies, big middle-aged bikers, were yelling and pushing into our circle. More people gathered at the periphery of their knot.

I couldn't see much, only a globe of dust and shouting. Beer splashed on the dirt and turned to mud, covered in bootprints. The bartender and one of the regulars came over and separated the men, but the fight would've died down anyway. It was obvious none of them had the stamina. Audrey handed me her beer.

"Help me finish this," she said. "Let's get out of here."

CHAPTER EIGHT

Audrey unlocked a red Honda Civic parked on the street. "You can throw that shit in the back," she said. I shoved aside magazines, clothes, shoes, and CDs, and sat. She steered into traffic on Alabama.

"How can you stand those guys?" I said.

"I hate them."

"I don't blame you. Jesus. What assholes."

"Danielle hated them, too. She was just really good at separating that from work. She was way better at it than me."

"Oh, god," I said, realizing. "You have to have sex with them, don't you."

"I'm done with those douche bags. Especially Anthony."

Audrey took a left.

"Where we going?" I asked.

"Shopping expedition. How much money do you have?"

"Uh . . ."

"Do you have forty dollars?"

"For what?"

"Coke. You like coke?"

I hadn't been around coke since the old days with Danielle. I loved it and I hated it, same as everybody.

"I have forty dollars," I said.

We sped north past the Loop, through neighborhoods and stretches of native forest. The cluster of pines and undergrowth gathered evening shadow. We passed subdivisions and people walking their retrievers in the twilight. The clouds glowed pink and purple in the sky.

"Fucking sunset," Audrey said.

"You don't like it?"

"I like night."

Who doesn't like sunsets? I thought. I studied her profile while she drove. She was agitated, her fingers moving on the steering wheel. She drove unsteadily, kept speeding up and slowing down.

"Where is this place?" I asked her.

"Almost there."

The sky settled into streetlights and tree shadows. Gradually Audrey relaxed next to me.

"You and Brandon are close, huh?" I said.

"We hang out a lot. The three of us, me, him, and Dani."

"That was very chivalrous," I said. "How he stood up for you."

"You mean the fight? He's not the first guy I've seen punch Anthony."

"I can see why," I said.

She turned into a parking lot flanked by pine forest on one side and a slapped-together apartment complex on the other.

"Come on," she said. "Give me the cash."

I handed it over. We walked across the asphalt to a set of stairs, and around a corner to a door where she stopped and sent a text message from her phone. Crickets sang from someplace close. She grinned at me. "This won't take long," she said.

The door opened and Audrey grabbed my wrist and hauled me inside. It was dim. Central air blew from a vent in a wall. A switch clicked on, and after a couple of flickers, harsh light invaded the room. It wasn't much of an improvement.

Our host had a flat pale face and fauxhawked hair. His grin made him adorable in the way of children in cookie commercials and when it departed it left him bereft, with an assortment of random features that didn't quite add up to a face. Veiny muscles showed through his shirt.

"Audrey, great to see you," he said, kissing her ear.

"Jacob," Audrey said, "this is Charlotte."

He took my hand and peered at us. "You could be sisters, couldn't you? Same eyebrows."

I glanced at Audrey. We didn't look at all alike. She shrugged.

"Sit down, sit down," the guy said.

He gestured to a couch in the corner, behind a wide glass-topped coffee table. On the table lay the fattest cat I'd ever seen. I skirted around it to take a seat on the couch. Cat hair grayed the green upholstery and flew out in a cloud as I sat.

"Jacob," Audrey said, "we can't stay long."

"I'll fix you a drink," he said.

He left for the kitchen and Audrey scooted closer to me.

"Check this out," she said. "It's amazing."

She picked up an unplugged lava lamp from the adjacent shelf and balanced it on the cat. She took her hands away. The lamp listed slightly to one side, but didn't fall. The cat lay still as though stuffed.

"I always do this," she said. "He likes it, I think. I put a bowl of cereal on him for an hour one time. He never moved."

We heard the whir of a machine from the kitchen, and Jacob emerged with three dark gray smoothies garnished with parsley stems. He set one in front of each of us.

"New juicer," he said. "It's amazing."

"Jacob, what the hell is in this?" Audrey asked.

"Uh, carrot. Beet. Pear. Blue-green algae. And a splash of rum. I invented it."

We took experimental sips.

"It's gross," Audrey said.

"It could use some salt," Jacob said. "I've also been making a meat drink for Oliver. He loves it."

He bounced into the kitchen again and returned carrying a ceramic salt shaker shaped like a fried egg, with two holes poked in the yolk. The condensation on the outside of my glass had attracted quite a lot of cat hair.

"J," Audrey said. "Do you have what you gave me before?"

"Right. Yes. Oliver, come on, old man. We need the table, here."

Jacob scooped his arms under the giant blob of cat and set him on the carpet. Oliver's head flopped to one side, but he seemed otherwise unaffected by his new location. After a minute he scooted towards the hall, surprisingly fast, his belly swaying between his legs. Meat juice.

"It's not what we had," Jacob said, "but it's good, very good."

He wiped the table with a wet rag and brought out a little bag of white powder. Audrey saw the damp swipes of cat hair on the table and dug in her purse for a tissue, which she licked and wiped across the glass. She dried the table carefully with the sleeve of her sweater, leaving a clean patch the size of a dinner plate.

"An oasis!" Jacob said.

He tapped the coke out. The harsh light made him look waxy. I could see Audrey's pores. She snorted a line and handed me the rolled bill. I did my line and let the rush creep and build, like fluorescent light in my bloodstream. The dim apartment,

Jacob and Audrey, everything took on a strange cast, refreshingly unfamiliar. I relaxed into it, waited to see what might happen. I could leave the past behind, make new friends. I felt better than I had since Michael dumped me.

Audrey was telling some story about this rich dude she knew who kept a polar bear cub for a pet in a climate-controlled room, and when the cub got too big he'd trade it in for a baby one.

"That's awful," I said.

"That's awesome," said Jacob. "A motherfucking polar bear?"

"What happens to the ones he gets rid of?" I said.

Audrey snorted another line and flipped her head up, blinking.

"Fuck," she said. "Don't ask me. I never met the bear."

"Who is this guy?" Jacob said.

"This asshole I met."

"An asshole who likes polar bears," Jacob said, impressed. "So it would have to be, what, ten degrees or some shit?"

"What?"

"The room, the room, the fucking room. For the motherfucking polar bears! The room. For the bear. Shit, y'all are high."

"I hate the cold," I said. "I hate air-conditioning. I don't even like fall."

Jacob said, "Anyway, polar bears aren't actual bears. It's a myth."

"They are, too," Audrey said. "You're thinking of panda bears."

"Or koala bears," I said.

Jacob looked dejected, then brightened. "Did you hear they discovered a new animal?" he said.

"The rich dude?" I said.

"Not the dude," Jacob said. "Scientists."

"What kind of animal?" Audrey said.

"It's a, like a lobster, except it's white. And it has hairs on it."

"Huh," I said.

"It's albino," Jacob said. "And blind." He lit a cigarette from my pack on the table.

"Where'd they find it?" I said.

"On the ocean floor someplace. It's supposedly ancient."

"Then it's not new," I said.

"Well, new to us," he said. "To people."

"It's vintage," I said, giggling.

Audrey stood and stretched. She picked up a CD and set it down.

"I can't sit still," she said, pacing the stained carpet. I was having the opposite problem. My pulse was racing but I felt sort of paralyzed on the couch.

"Do you have any more of this stuff?" I asked, holding my glass.

"You're really cool," Jacob said, and took the glass into the kitchen.

"Uh, thanks," I said.

Audrey wandered down the hall and I peeked in the tiny yellowed kitchen, where Jacob was banging around. An old brown stove held a board piled high with appliances: blender, food processor, juicer, an espresso machine, a couple of gadgets I didn't recognize. Jacob stood at the sink.

"You cook a lot?" I said.

"I like machines," he said. "That's awesome you came over."

I wondered if he sold drugs as a way to get people to hang out with him. I leaned against the wall and immediately stood upright; it was sticky. Jacob wrestled with an oversized carrot, thick and long as my arm.

Audrey appeared in the doorway. "We have to go," she said.

"Not yet," Jacob said. "Stay."

"Sorry," I told him. I grabbed my sweater and bag and we

went out to the car. Now that I was outside I realized how depressing it was in there. Audrey drove back the way we'd come, took a right onto the feeder road, and gained entrance to the freeway. I was still thinking of the sticky wall.

"How do you know that guy?" I said.

"Jacob used to go out with a girl I used to dance with. I never understood why she liked him. Let's get a drink."

"Yes," I said.

We stopped at a beverage mart with plate-glass windows, half of them covered in plywood. We bought whiskey, cigarettes, and two Diet Cokes. Audrey guided the car around the building, away from the security lights, and we did a couple more lines. Her eyes glittered. I was aware, looking at her, that I had never been in this particular situation before. That whatever was happening was happening for the first time. She leaned back and stuck her feet out the window. Her legs were slender and tan. She looked like a fantasy of carefree summertime, and I remembered why we were there: Danielle was dead. I guess Audrey was thinking the same thing.

"Last week," she said, "we were hanging out at Brandon's looking at magazines. Watching cable. We got some takeout Chinese. She always ordered this slimy eggplant. It's her favorite. And now she's—" Audrey took a long breath. "Now she's nowhere."

"I know," I said.

"So where the fuck did she go?" Audrey said.

"It makes no sense," I said. "Shit like this, it doesn't just happen. Not to Danielle."

"It did, though," she said.

"Who do you think did it?" I said.

Audrey shuddered. "I can't think about that. I get too freaked out."

"Aren't you scared?" I asked her. "Like those girls who weren't at the service?"

"Those girls hardly knew Danielle. They're being all dramatic. They're probably glad she's dead because she was way hotter than them."

"You don't think it could be some stalker who likes your videos?"

"Shit. Now you're *trying* to scare me."

"No," I said, "I'm sorry."

We watched a mosquito brushing the windshield.

"It wants to get out," Audrey said. "It's tired, it's not even biting us." With her thumb she mashed the bug against the glass. "I hate this," she said. "Let's drive."

She took a swig of whiskey and handed me the bottle, then brought her legs in the car and shifted it into gear. Drunkenness rolled over the edges of my body.

Audrey fiddled with the radio. "Come on, where's a fucking song? I can't stand how these DJs talk. Why can't they talk like normal people?"

I took over the dial and found some music. We cranked it loud and floated along the freeway. Smog cushioned the air, cradled us.

"I feel bad," Audrey said. "I never went in the church. I was going to. I just couldn't."

"I don't think she'd care," I said. "It wasn't exactly her style."

"You're trying to cheer me up. You're sweet."

"I mean it, too, though," I said. "That was her mom's deal, completely."

I thought of all those people—adults with money and suits. I wondered how many of them actually knew Danielle. Then again, maybe I didn't know her, either. Not really, not anymore.

We exited the freeway and rolled through a neighborhood

of quiet houses, clean and well lit, the buildings set close to the street inside high fences. Audrey glanced at me and smiled. Tears had smudged her eyeliner. It made her look more tangible somehow.

"Where are we?" I said.

She shrugged.

"You're good at driving around," I said.

"What?"

"I can't do it, I'm always too anxious, like I have to know the next turn."

"There's not much to it," she said. "If you don't care, you can't make a mistake."

This seemed profound to me and I was quiet. She took a left down a street that ended in a cul-de-sac. We turned around and she tried a different street, and another. They kept circling and we saw more quiet townhomes, more gates, more fake old-fashioned oil lamps on the fences. I felt jangly, disconnected, like where we were had nothing to do with me. I watched us like a commercial, because it was on.

"Hey," she said. "A park."

Up the block lay an expanse of green, a stone table, a swing set and jungle gym. The playground looked enchanted, marked by white light from the lamps along a paved path. My face ached from the coke. We walked on brown mulch, twisting our ankles in our high-heeled shoes, and huddled on the ground by the metal slide. The night was warm and windless. Audrey measured out two fat lines on the flat part of the slide. Her lips curved up at the corners, setting her dimples in shadow. She pulled her hair back with one hand, eyes shining black in the sodium light. We snorted the lines.

"Come on," she said.

She ran to the swing set. I left our rolled dollar bill on the slide and followed her. We each took a swing and soon we were breathless, pumping with our legs. Audrey's shoe flew off at the top of her arc and banged the merry-go-round with a metal clang. We waited to see if it woke any of the neighbors. No sign came from the houses.

"Swing, swang, swung," Audrey chanted. I tried to get in sync with her. The chains of her swing ran parallel to the ground, she was that high.

"I love swings," I said. "How come I never swing anymore?"

"Because," Audrey said. "There's always fucking kids around."

"You're right," I said, laughing. "That's exactly it."

"I bet I can jump past the sidewalk," Audrey said.

"Be careful," I said, but she was already airborne. She landed in a crouch, on her feet, a yard or two short of the path, and leapt up and did a cartwheel.

"I used to be a cheerleader," she said. "Were you a cheerleader? Let's do cheers."

"I never went to a game," I said. "I smoked and listened to the Smiths."

Audrey ignored me. She did another cartwheel. Her flared skirt fell up, revealing a lacy thong. On her feet, she began an elaborate series of motions, finishing with her arms outstretched. She chanted, "Win! Win! Wildcats! Whoo!"

"That's cute," I said. I let my feet scuff the dirt. "Did you have a little outfit?"

"I had two," she said. "Green and gold, and white with green and gold trim. And pompoms. I was very popular."

I swung higher. I felt great.

"I never did coke except with Danielle," I said.

"What happened?"

"Nothing. We got high."

"I mean with you and her," she said.

"We grew apart, I guess. She was different back then. You never knew her when she was doing heroin."

"I've been around it, though, with other people. It's so gross."

"Yeah. I wasn't into it and she was. It was like she just dedicated her whole life to getting high. She didn't care about anything else, and she wouldn't try to quit. I wanted to help her, but nothing I did seemed to make a difference."

"I can't picture her like that," Audrey said.

"It was such a long time ago. I'm glad I got to see her last week. She was doing great. At least it seemed that way to me."

"She loved seeing you, too."

"Really?" I said.

Audrey sat on the swing again. "Yeah, she was excited. She talked about you all through dinner, how you guys used to do everything together, and how you were super smart and such a good friend. She could not believe you wanted to give her that money."

"I can't believe she didn't take it," I said.

"I know, she's such a weirdo. She really hates her mom."

"Yeah. Always has."

"It was super nice of you. You didn't even have to get in touch with her. You went out of your way to see her."

"Yeah. Well. I care about her," I said.

I think we both realized at the same time that we were using present tense. Danielle was dead. It seemed so unfair and unbudging. I felt tears forming.

"Fuck," I said, trying to breathe and not cry.

Audrey grabbed on to the chain of my swing, jerking us both in erratic diagonals. I put my feet down to stop the motion. Our swings finally stilled, and we sat quietly like that, each of us occasionally sniffling. We looked out at the moonlit park.

After a few minutes Audrey spoke. "What I don't get," she said, "is why you quit doing coke. It's fucking awesome."

I started to laugh. I had an urge to hurl myself off the swing like Audrey had done, for the pleasure of being in the air. We went to the slide and did lines, Audrey in one sweep, breathing it in like air, and me in stages, shuddering and gasping. The aluminum slide glowed like a piece of moonlight striped with snow. I looked at her long fingers, steady and precise, and her neck as she bent over the lines with the dollar bill. I lit a cigarette.

She said, "There's a guy who lives in one of these neighborhoods like this, with all new houses. Him and his wife. I think he had kids, too. You ever get involved with a married dude?"

"No."

"I got tired of it after a while. Danielle always said, you deserve someone all to yourself. I liked him, though. He had a big dick."

I giggled. She handed me the bill and moved aside. The coke made me twitch. It tasted like dirty dishwater. After I did the line, Audrey licked the flat of her palm, wiped it over the slide, and tongued the coke residue off her hand.

"Gross," I said. "Little kids' butts touch that."

"You're such a girl," she said.

"Want to take a walk?" I said. The playground mulch hurt my feet, and I had begun to feel trapped inside the park. We put on our shoes and walked along the path until it met the street. Cockroaches flew around the lamps. The road curved along, tidy, lined with identical houses.

"These kinds of neighborhoods always weird me out," I said.

"I think they're great. Not dirty yet, or broken. I always wished I could live in a place like this. Perfectly clean and new."

At this hour, under the soft streetlights, we strolled along the center of the smooth blacktop. The garish façades and silly gardens stayed in shadow, the whole street tucked in, safe. I could see what Audrey meant. We circled around the neighborhood and arrived again at the little park. My head hurt from the coke and whiskey. I wanted to go home.

In the car Audrey turned the way we came and entered the freeway.

"Where do you live?" she asked me.

"You should take me to my car. I left it at the funeral."

"Jesus, the funeral. Was that today?"

"Well, yesterday. Technically."

The sky softened into dawn around the buildings, and more cars filled the freeway. I felt tired of being so awake. We got on 59 and exited at Shepherd, making our way to the church. She parked next to my car in the overflow lot, empty now.

"Thanks," I said. "We should do this again."

"Yeah, definitely," she said.

We exchanged phone numbers and I hugged her. I felt good, almost, for the first time since all this started. I realized I hadn't thought about Michael once. I drove home and fell asleep in the morning sun.

CHAPTER NINE

I didn't wake up until late afternoon. I sat at the window over-looking the street. A dog who lived by the roadside gnawed on some garbage, and the neighbor girl sat on her stoop talk-ing with her girlfriends, occasionally calling to her kid inside watching TV. I opened a beer. I felt peaceful, dampened by alco-hol and drugs, and less alone after the night with Audrey.

I slept again and woke early the next morning, energy surging through me. I went for a long run, sweating as soon as I stepped outside. A night rain had washed the city and it gleamed in May's sun and sharp shadows. The mornings were a few degrees cooler, but the dew hadn't burned off yet, leav-ing the air dense and wet. Mallards with their iridescent necks dotted the pond. I couldn't see any of the little dark ducks, the ones I liked. I guessed they were still tucked in their nests. I kept going.

I did five miles, barely noticing—I never felt like stopping. I crossed Main near the roundabout and had to sprint to avoid a car. At the other side I fell into a rhythm, a phrase repeating in my head. Danielle is dead Danielle is dead Danielle is dead.

I couldn't understand the transformation from beautiful Danielle to that bloody mess in the motel room. Somebody did that to her, and now he was out driving around, eating sandwiches or whatever. She must have met someone there at the motel. A john. Or maybe Anthony or one of those porn guys, models or whatever they called themselves. She'd walked into that room, thinking she was safe. Maybe it was random—wrong place, wrong time.

Danielle and I used to play mermaids in the pool, a game she'd made up as a kid, long before I knew her. You had to swim with your legs together as though you had a tail, and try to be sexy. Not much of a game, really, just something silly to do if we were bored. She used to surprise me like that. One minute working out a plan to score drugs, or talking shit about some poor kid at school, and a minute later she'd say, "Let's play mermaids!" Excited and sincere as an eight-year-old girl.

Light poured through the leaves over the shady path surrounding Rice University, yellowing and weakening the green. I passed a few people on the trail. Usually I smiled at the other joggers, acknowledging the folly of running in ninety-degree weather. Now I couldn't meet their eyes. I picked up speed until I didn't have the breath to cry. I got off the path and turned into the street, where people would be safely in their air-conditioned cars and houses. I ran, pure speed and rhythm: Danielle-is-dead-Danielle-is-dead.

I fantasized about a sip of water, and I wanted it so bad it blocked out all my other thoughts. I headed home, in a state of consuming thirst, aware of an ache in my left heel. At home I didn't drink at first because I feared when the thirst disappeared that I would, too. I lay on the floor to let my body cool down, listening to my heartbeat.

I drank some water and tidied each room, scrubbed and

dried the kitchen floor. I sorted my dirty laundry by color and pulled out the clothes that needed to be hand-washed. I cleaned the sink and filled it with Woolite and water, let the pieces soak. I relaxed seeing my clean apartment draped in drying lingerie, sweaters, and skirts. I showered and dressed, put on makeup—I had a way of doing it where I didn't have to see my whole face—one eye, then the other, cheekbones, lips. I looked like my mother and I couldn't deal with that today.

I had this impulse to be around the people who knew Danielle. They were the only ones who could understand what this was like. I called Audrey but she didn't pick up, so I looked up the address of Houston Mediasource, where Brandon worked. Its offices were in a big old house on a cul-de-sac under the downtown spur of 59. I realized I'd passed by it a million times and never realized what it was. I drove there and parked in the lot, a yard that had been asphalted over. Dandelions and grasses struggled through its many cracks. Dirt blossomed over the white stucco, and dusky blue paint peeled from the window frames. I stepped into a tiny room containing a large desk and shelves with a mess of coiled wires. The place showed its dust and age. A girl sat behind the desk, untangling some cables. I told her I was there to see Brandon Young.

She led me into the living room, which had been carved into offices. The tiny space had kept the original ceiling, high above us. It was like standing in an elevator or a deep well. We walked through a hallway, a kitchen, a breezeway that had been added to join the house to a double-wide trailer. I knocked on the open door. Brandon glanced up from his computer screen.

"Hi," I said. "We met—"

"Charlotte. I remember." His eyes were red.

"Could we talk?" I asked. "If you're not busy?"

He shrugged and gestured to a chair in front of his desk.

The furniture looked like it had come from a surplus store. Light from the windows emphasized the plasticky walls, the clutter everywhere. A broken staple glinted in the industrial carpet. Brandon slumped behind his desk, a pen in one hand.

"This place isn't quite what I expected," I said.

"Everyone says that," he said. "People think it will be a slick studio." He patted the desk in front of him, in apology or consolation. "What are you doing here?"

"I don't know," I said. "I wanted—I wanted to talk to somebody who knew her."

"Yeah. I know what you mean."

"I can't believe she's dead."

He rubbed one hand over his face. The phone on his desk rang. He stared like he didn't recognize it. We listened to it ring and then stop ringing. He said, "I need a fucking drink. You can come if you want."

We caravanned to the Spanish Flower and parked our cars side by side. He took a booth and we ordered frozen margaritas. A black-haired girl wearing a flamenco costume dropped off our basket of chips.

I said, "That fight at the icehouse—that was dramatic."

"Anthony. Jesus. Not my best moment."

"It was perfect, actually. He was being a dick."

"I bruised my hand." He showed me his knuckles, swollen and healing a greenish-blue. "I had to make him shut the fuck up. He's got no sense of decorum."

"Didn't he work for you?"

"Not after that. Those guys are dispensable."

We both winced at the word. I thought, That's two he'll have to replace. Our drinks came. He fiddled with his straw, threw it on the table, and gulped a third of his glass.

"Do people at your job know you make pornography?" I asked.

"I don't think so. Even if they did, I think most of them would be okay with it. I've been there a long time, and they're fairly open-minded. They're artists, or they think they are. And they respect me. They're very supportive of my other films."

"What are your films like?" I asked.

"Experimental. Like collages. I'm working on one now that incorporates audio from drivers' ed instructional videos and images from video games, plus a bunch of macro footage of an ant farm that I shot last year. It's close to being done."

"Cool," I said.

"I've had films in a few festivals. And Mediasource is great—I get to use their equipment. Plus I believe in community television. A lot of it's crap, but it's an important vehicle of expression for students and young filmmakers."

"I wish I had something like that," I said. "Art, or something I cared about."

"What do you do?" he said.

"I'm a barista," I said. "Impressive, right?"

"Nothing wrong with that," he said.

"I guess. I might go back to school, I don't know. I should try to save up and take some classes."

"The porn is how I'm paying off my student loans. That's why I got into it. Not a lot of money in experimental film. Or community television."

"What's it like, making porn?"

"It's easy. Anybody can build a website. And it's fun. Mostly."

"Mostly?"

"Well, the people aren't always the most stable group, emotionally. Or, like, showing up for work. Personalities to deal with, egos, drugs, shit like that."

"How did Danielle deal with being around drugs? I got the impression she avoided all that."

"It didn't bother her. She smoked weed a little. She never did meth, like some of them did. I had to make a rule, no meth on set or you're fired. It's tough for them—I understand it, why they want to get high. But when they're spun they act like a bunch of three-year-olds. Complaining, demanding attention. Danielle had a sense of humor about it. You have to, basically, to stay in it for long."

"Could any of those guys have hurt Danielle?"

"I've thought about it and thought about it. I don't think so. They're pussies, when it comes down to it. They never tried to stand up to her. I mean, she was so confident, and sweet. They respected her. I have no idea who could've killed her."

"Even if they were cranked up? Even Anthony?"

"It's hard to imagine . . . any of it. I keep thinking she'll walk through the door."

I looked towards the door. It was easy to imagine her there, her hair shining, a smirk on her face. Brandon picked a cold tortilla chip from the basket and dropped it. It broke in half on top of the other chips and settled in, camouflaged among its brothers and sisters.

"You know," I said, "I hung out with her one time in the last two years. Two days later, she was dead."

"Jesus."

"I keep thinking it's my fault, somehow. I know that doesn't make sense."

"Well, did you kill her?"

"No. Of course not."

"There you go, then."

"How long were y'all together?" I asked.

"About four months. But it's not like she was my girlfriend. We fucked. Everybody fucks everybody."

"She liked you," I said.

"Yeah? What'd she say?"

"That you're a good guy. You're talented. She told me you're going to be big, you're going to make real movies."

"She said that?"

He leaned forward, eager for this little piece of information. I nodded. Tiny details became so important when nothing else was left.

"It's crazy," he said. "One day she was there, and the next day, cops are everywhere, her makeup's still all over the bathroom like she's coming home any second, they're telling me she's . . ."

He stopped speaking, let his sentence collapse.

"Yeah," I said. "It's impossible to get a handle on it."

"I miss her," he said. "But that's not the worst. How she died—it's horrible."

"Let's get another round," I said. I signaled to the waitress.

"Can I ask you a question?" he said. "Are the cops talking to you?"

"That detective did," I said. "Ash."

"They keep coming to my house and the office, and calling me. They think I fucking killed her. They keep asking me, where was I, had we fought, they keep talking about old shit."

"Like what?"

"This bar fight I got into a long time ago. I was twenty-two. It was dumb. Some fratty assholes were picking on this kid, this friend of mine. I threw a punch and the police showed up. One of the dudes had a knife and they arrested everyone."

I thought of the other punch, that I had witnessed. He caught my look.

"I have a temper," he said. "I admit it. But I've never hit a woman. I could never hurt Danielle."

I sipped my drink, keeping my eyes on him.

"Do you believe me?" he said.

"Yeah."

He smiled at me and I smiled back. His sorrow gave me an odd sense of comfort, and it felt good to be there, drinking.

"You and Audrey been hanging out?" he said.

"Only once, the other night. I met her before, with Danielle."

"They were best friends. The three of us hung around together a lot. They were great to work with, too. Their videos are popular."

"I like Audrey," I said.

"Yeah, Audrey's okay. I like her, too. I don't think she'll stick around, though. I mean the guys were douchey to her, you saw it. Except when Danielle was there. Now . . . it will be different now."

"Everything is different now," I said.

"I keep remembering random things. One night I stayed late to finish a project at work, and I didn't get home until nine o'clock. She'd ordered a pizza for me. She kept it hot in the oven. Shit like that, that's nice. Most people, you get to know them, no matter how normal or cool they come off at first, underneath they're needy, or crazy, or delusional. D, she was always smiling, doing her nails, whatever. You could trust her."

"That's great to hear. She really was doing okay, wasn't she?"

"Yeah. She didn't talk to me much about her past. I had the sense things were bad."

"It *was* bad. I mean, she was still Danielle, she could make everything seem fun, and like you were the most amazing person. But with the drugs, she was angry a lot, and she didn't really care about anybody. She was just kind of checked out all the time, didn't pay attention to anything. It sucked. I'm so glad she got clean."

"I just can't imagine her like that," Brandon said.

"You're lucky you got to spend time with her when you did," I said. "Maybe you saw her at her best. I never had the chance to get to know her again."

Brandon reached out his hand, the bruised one, and rubbed the sweat from his glass across my knuckles. At his touch, tears came to my eyes. He slid out of the booth and sat next to me. I leaned against him, and he held me. He looked tired, his forehead marked by fine wrinkles, like pencil lines that had been erased. We sipped our margaritas, huddled together, stunned by grief.

"What time is it?" he said.

"Seven," I said, glancing at my phone.

"Fucking happy hour's over," he said. "Let's go to my place." He rose and tossed a bill on the table, downed the rest of his drink standing up.

He lived six blocks away, on the other side of Main, in a neighborhood of bungalows across from a park. The dog walkers were out, still dressed for the office, carrying plastic bags of poop. I parked my car behind his on the street. He had the whole place to himself, a two-bedroom, cute, painted blue. The arched front door led into a living room/dining room decorated with a combination of Ikea and thrift-store furniture.

"Sit down," he said. "Be right back."

He walked past the large table to the kitchen and returned with his arms full: a bong, a ceramic plate, and two glasses filled with ice and vodka.

He sat beside me and reached under the coffee table for a box. He rummaged through its contents and laid out a pill bottle, a razor blade, a straw, and a tiny bag of white powder.

"What is that?" I said.

"Special K," he said. "Ever done it?"

"I don't think so," I said.

He opened the pill bottle, full of buds, and loaded the bong. He pushed it in front of me. I fished a lighter from my pocket.

"Since Danielle died, I can't be sober," he said.

"I know what you mean," I said.

I tucked my hair behind my ears and leaned over the bong. I had to use my hand to seal the wide opening. Brandon smashed the powder on the plate and formed lines. The high built gently as my body began to sense itself. The room grew cozy. I kicked off my shoes and sat cross-legged on the couch, facing him while he smoked.

"Do you ever get tired of sex?" I asked. "Filming it all day?"

"Are you kidding?" he said. "Never. I think about it all the fucking time."

I laughed. "What was she like, in bed?"

"Playful. Sweet."

"Like how?"

"When we fucked, she smiled at me, touched my face. Like there was no one she'd rather be with."

I nodded. I knew that, how she could make you feel that way.

"It was nice," he said, "but she was always removed from it. She never let go, never got *naked*. That's not what I like the best. I like sex to be . . . desperate. To fuck . . ."

"Like it matters," I said. "Like you have to."

"Yeah. She never had that. I mean, we were friends, we weren't in love. What sucks is we had a fight."

"What, you and Danielle?"

"Yeah, the night she died. If I had known that was it, I would never—I should have stayed out of her business."

"What did you fight about?

"The inheritance. It was after she met with her mother. Her mom wanted to buy the land—"

"What land?"

"You know, her inheritance."

"I figured it was money. Or antiques maybe. Sally never said anything to me about it."

"No, there was an acreage. Danielle got one parcel of it and her mom got the rest. Her mom offered her three hundred grand. And Danielle wouldn't sell."

"Wow. I had no idea."

My body flashed hot and cold, leaving goose bumps on my arms. How could Sally not have told me? It made no sense. Brandon was still talking and I tried to concentrate.

"I thought Danielle was nuts," he said. "I mean, three hundred thousand dollars, can you imagine? She said I didn't get it. Her mom was the most selfish person in the world, she could never trust her."

"What else did she say?"

"That her mom used money to get whatever she wanted. Danielle refused to be bought. But with that much money she could buy a house, go to school, whatever. She could have financed my business, we could have expanded, made some serious cash. She wouldn't listen to me. She was mad. I told her what I thought—I didn't know it was that big a deal. We never argued before, not once. She yelled at me for half an hour, then she packed a bag of clothes and left. I figured she'd call and apologize."

"Then she went to the motel?"

"Yeah. I guess. She must have. I never saw her again."

I could see why the cops kept questioning him. But they should be talking to Sally, not him.

"You look pale," he said. "Smoke some more."

He reloaded the bong and lit it for me. I inhaled the smoke and held it.

"She was so upset," Brandon said. "I wish I'd stayed out of it."

He took a ragged breath and wept quietly, trembling, baring the depth of his heartache, his exhaustion. At my touch he clung to me, and for a second I hated Danielle for dying and hurting everyone, making everyone sad.

"Charlotte," he said. "Thanks for being here with me."

"Of course," I said. "It makes me feel better, too."

He straightened, but left his knee touching mine. The connection between us grew like the slow filling of a pitcher, a simple promise I knew would be kept. I quit thinking about Sally and Danielle and thought about his leg against mine, and how he needed me. We hit the bong again, though I was already high. He busied himself with the white powder on the plate and snorted half.

"Try this," he said. "It's not a lot. It won't send you into a hole, it just takes you away a little."

The white grains stood out on the red plate, like a flag of some fucked-up country. He stroked my hair while I snorted the K. He touched the straps of my tank top, the hem of my skirt. There was a cavalier quality about it that thrilled me. His fingers moved from the fabric to my skin, and I felt such gratitude and warmth. I would do what he wanted, I didn't care what.

"You're beautiful," he said.

Not like her, I thought. Nonetheless I liked his words and his hands on me. I made a decision then to let her in, to let her live inside me. I'd let in the dead, her and my mom; they could have me. I'd empty myself to make room. As soon as I had the thought it started happening. My self evaporated. In our kiss he bit me hard, and my body twitched, and they were right there, all the people I'd never see again. He tightened his grip on my thigh and leaned over me. My legs parted as he kissed my cheek, my neck, my lips. I smelled an odd, chemical odor about him. I held him to me. He sucked the air out of my lungs and I was glad; I didn't need it anymore. I needed room.

"God, I miss her," he mumbled.

He was doing it, too: channeling the dead. I understood and the understanding flew between us every place we touched.

Simultaneously I felt curious, analytical and without agency. I waited to see what would happen. Maybe it was the drugs, making me separate from my body, or the presence of Danielle inside me, in both of us, or maybe it was his cock, thick and hard and curved at the tip, the way he gained confidence, shed his grief as he entered me, turned me over and fucked me from behind, yanking my hair, holding me with his arm around my neck, pumping steadily, filling me and pulling out and filling me again. I came three times from fucking, and my body disappeared. I could see it on the end of his cock, a separate thing, pulsing like a severed lizard's tail—disposable, controlled by a distant electricity. I think for a while I stopped breathing. Pieces of him ended up under my nails.

I can't remember when it stopped or even if he came. At some point I was in the car, driving, having to learn again how to control my limbs to steer and brake and accelerate. I attached no emotion to any of these processes. Everything still seemed inconsequential and also fine.

CHAPTER TEN

The next day I put on a sundress and made coffee. I thought I'd be more affected by the K, but I felt normal, like it had happened to somebody else. I liked being with Danielle's friends. I could relax around them, like they'd been preapproved. My computer lay open, sleeping, and when I moved the mouse the screen brightened, still showing the porn site. What the hell, I thought, and played the video I'd seen before, of Danielle and Audrey together.

Audrey wore a simple shift that hung loosely, showing her body through the sheer fabric. Her slender back and bare feet and the way she moved, deliberately, with her eyes open wide, didn't mesh with Danielle's bratty cartoon appeal. The two women kissed, turning for the camera. Audrey sat on a bench and Danielle knelt over her, pushing her thigh between Audrey's legs.

How could her death exist in the same world as this tacky video? It was impossible, nonsensical. I wept and kept watching. Audrey reached to touch Danielle's face. They smiled at each other, genuine. I felt a vibration in my sinuses and deep in my joints, an inaudible singing, like missing every place I'd ever been—every room, every park, every street I'd driven down in my whole life. I longed for them all at once, astonished at the pain, the inability to access the past. Usually I never knew what to want. Now suddenly I wanted everything. The world rushed from me, like each moment of the wanting had already ended by the time I perceived it. I was helpless to make it stay.

A man entered the frame and the girls turned to him. He was one of the ones I met. Kenneth, maybe? I couldn't remember his name. One of the other guys came in and I watched the rest absentmindedly, a series of acrobatic permutations among the four of them.

I thought of the photos of Danielle's body. Someone had beaten her until she stopped moving, and kept hitting her until her head caved in. I pressed my hands to my face, felt the hardness of my own skull. I couldn't fathom the passion, the energy it would take to break a person's head. What had Danielle done to make someone that crazy? She and Brandon had fought, but I believed his story. I couldn't see him following her to the motel. It really bothered me that Sally hadn't told me about the land. Or about seeing Danielle. She could have mentioned it. There was no reason not to.

I decided to talk to Sally again. Something weird was going on and I had a bad feeling that I was in the middle of it. The day was hot and breezy. I took my bike out. I rode on the sidewalk, wound through patched parking lots and bayou trails and walled streets lined with maples, the tops of townhomes visible beyond them. In River Oaks the streets were shaded by live oaks whose branches formed a canopy above the road. The neighborhood felt a couple of degrees cooler than the rest of the city. How did they do that? Were they air-conditioning the outside?

I rounded the corner of Sally's block and stopped in front of her house, watching the Mexican workers mowing the neighbor's grass and carrying bags of mulch from their trucks. I walked my bike up Sally's drive and through the gate, past the outdoor room where we'd sat the other night. The pool threw off shards of light. A few leaves floated near the tiled sides, and a leggy begonia in a pot drooped, touching the water. Red caladiums rustled under a drake elm, and large pots filled with bamboo lined the side of the yard. A couple of spindly lemon trees shed sparse leaves onto the mulch below. A voice startled me.

"Charlotte? Sweetheart. Come on in."

Sally stood in the entrance to the screened patio. I'd meant to confront her about the land, find out about the fight they'd had, but she looked so grateful to see me I couldn't say a word. I let her lead me inside, through the dining room's French doors. The room I remembered had been a rich coffee color. She'd repainted the walls red. I liked it better before. The table shone with wax.

"I'll fix us some iced tea," Sally said from the kitchen. "It's hot out there. Are you hungry? There's leftovers from the caterer—artichokes, some grilled shrimp—I'll make a plate. This shrimp is delish. Wait till you try it."

I sat on a stool at the kitchen counter while Sally dished out food. She poured tea into tumblers and added lemon wedges. We carried our plates into the breakfast nook. It disoriented me to be at the table, sharing a meal with her. Like I was in high school again, and Danielle was pouting in the other room, and my mom was alive, at home. I took a bite of shrimp.

"This is good," I said. I'd been forgetting to eat lately.

"I'm glad you dropped by."

I didn't know what to say. I was finding it hard to confront her.

"I miss her," she said.

"Me, too," I said.

"I mean, I've been missing her for years."

I blinked, surprised. Sally had always pretended everything was fine, even when Danielle used to scream at her. She'd smile at me and say, "Oh, teenagers," like I wasn't one, and ask me about school.

Sally said, "The other day I didn't tell you how much I appreciated you. If you hadn't put us in touch, I wouldn't have gotten to see her again."

"It was nothing," I said.

"I'm grateful for it," she said. "I'm so thankful. If I had known it would be the last time . . . I don't know."

"What happened?" I said.

Maybe Sally was finally going to talk honestly to me. She stood and poured more tea, and when she turned around I saw her mask was back up.

"We had a great dinner—paella from that place out on Bellaire," she said. "Have you tried it? It's exactly like what I had in Spain. And they have that Serrano ham."

"I meant how was Danielle?" I said.

"Oh, fine. She looked healthy, don't you think? Not too skinny. We talked about Aunt Baby. I used to take Danielle out there for visits. Those two adored each other. They baked cookies together and invented these silly dances. It was the cutest."

"I can't imagine Danielle doing that stuff," I said.

"Want to see some pictures? I had them out to show her. Let's go in the den."

We used to watch TV in the den. New couches of dark leather

anchored the Persian rug. Sally adjusted the wooden shutters to let some light in.

"You've changed the room around," I said.

"Oh, of course. I get tired of the same old stuff."

She pulled a suede-covered photo album off the shelf and sat beside me. We opened it on our laps. Sure enough, there was little Danielle in a kitchen with an older woman. They both had chocolate cake batter around their mouths and the woman was grinning. Another picture showed Danielle in pigtails sitting astride a brown pony, clearly thrilled. We flipped the pages, studying each image of this lovely child in jeans and pink tees. It must have been before the thing happened with her uncle. I'd never seen Danielle smile like that.

"How old was she here?" I said.

"About nine. A couple years after this we stopped going out there. Baby had a stroke, and she couldn't get around. We had to sell the animals. She said to me once, 'It's hell getting old.' I didn't think it was healthy for Danielle to be around that kind of attitude. Her life hadn't really turned out how she wanted, and then when her health declined she was so bitter. And she couldn't ride. Danielle would've gotten bored."

The next page contained pictures of the land, farmhouse and fences.

"Hard to believe," Sally said. "Now this is surrounded by development. Back then it was all horse pastures and cane fields."

"Is this the land Baby left to her?" I said.

"Yes. Danielle's parcel is adjacent to my six acres."

"What are you going to do with it?"

"I'm putting together a mixed commercial-residential development—we're ready to break ground as soon as it clears probate."

"You've had this planned? What, have you been waiting around for your aunt to die?"

"Come on, sweetie. I took care of Baby. She was dying for years. It simply made sense."

"That's why you tried to buy Danielle's share. You need it for your development."

"Well, partly. But she had to sell. Think what Danielle would have done with four acres in the middle of Tomball. Can you see her maintaining it, getting it Bush Hogged, paying property taxes?"

"I guess not," I said.

"Let me refill your tea," Sally said.

"I don't want any more," I said. I wanted a real drink, but I wasn't going to ask. "What happened when she told you she wanted to keep the land?"

"How do you know about all this, anyway? Did she talk to you about it?"

"Her friend told me," I said. "I know she was upset."

"She needed some time to think it over. She called me later. I had offered her three hundred for it and she countered with four, plus a two-point share in the profits."

I wasn't sure I believed her. Why would Danielle change her mind? It didn't make sense, just to hold out for more money. Danielle never cared about money.

"A two-point share? How much would that be?" I said.

"Oh, two or three hundred more, depending on the market."

With Danielle dead, that was over half a million dollars that Sally had saved. I stared at the photo album, unable to bring my eyes into focus. I felt hot in the air-conditioned room. My pulse beat in my temples.

Sally was still talking. "She stuck to her guns, she was a good negotiator. It made me proud of her. She could have been a fine businesswoman. I was going to help her invest the money, set it up in a trust."

"A trust," I echoed. Funny word. "Now what happens?"

"The land will be in probate a while, then it will revert to me."

I nodded, tried to swallow.

"Why didn't you tell me?" I said. "About the land, about your plans?"

"I don't know," Sally said. "I didn't think it mattered. It wasn't exactly your business."

"Well, it mattered," I said.

"Why, honey? What difference does it make?"

"Sally, you used me. If I had known—"

"Used you? Charlotte, I paid you. Besides, you just said it was nothing. A phone number."

"Would you have even bothered getting in touch with her if you didn't want the land for yourself?"

"Honey," she said, "Don't be like this. I haven't done anything wrong."

"Forget it," I said. "I don't want to hear it."

Sally sighed. "I wish things hadn't been so hard," she said. "Danielle was such a sweet little girl. Around when she turned twelve or so . . . well, puberty is always difficult, those hormones. And I guess she blamed me for the divorce."

"No, she didn't," I said. "I mean, maybe, but she got over that."

"Of course you didn't know her then."

"Sally, stop pretending. It was because of your brother."

"She talked to you about that?"

"Well, I was her *friend*." The last word came out vicious. Sally didn't seem to notice. She sat on the edge of the couch, twisting her sapphire ring with the other hand.

"She didn't tell me until after he moved back to Denver," she said.

"She told you and you still saw him, still let him in your house. Her house."

"Charlotte, what was I supposed to do? He flew in from Colorado. I didn't even know he was coming, he just showed up for dinner. Was I supposed to send him away at the door?"

"Yes," I said. "That is exactly what you were supposed to do."

"Gary and I had just split up," she said. "I was trying to keep our lives normal, to have a regular Thanksgiving, with people around."

"Fine, but not him," I said.

"It would have caused a scene. We had—Jesus, I had colleagues here. Investors. I told him that weekend not to come back. Gary took off, left town with his bimbo, I had to make the money—"

"A scene," I said, disgusted. "That's what you cared about?"

"Look, my own brother . . . we grew up together. I knew him. I mean, it was hard to believe."

"She didn't make it up," I said.

"I know that now. But back then, Charlotte, she hated me. She lied about everything. I wasn't sure. There was so much else going on. Danielle would never let it go."

"How could she? Nobody gets over something like that. Jesus. She was a little girl."

"I know," Sally said. "Of course you're right. But what could I do? By the time I found out, it was already over."

"Sally, she was completely alone. How can you not see that? You let him in your house, and she knew you didn't care about her."

"I did care. She's my child. Of course I cared. You know I sent her to therapy as soon as she told me what happened. I found the best doctors. But she lied to them, too, she just made up nonsense, or sometimes she wouldn't speak at all. We tried medication, antidepressants, but she refused to take them. She wouldn't let me help. She was so difficult. She specifically tried to antagonize me."

"Can you blame her?" I said.

"It's funny," Sally said. "I gave her everything I had, and she didn't care. Look how wonderful you turned out. I should have sent her to live with *your* mom."

I gaped at her, said nothing. It didn't deserve a response.

"Charlotte, I'm sorry," she said after a minute.

She rose and tried to hug me. I stood there, holding my breath, and as soon as she let go I ran out the door. I rode fast out of that neighborhood, trying to keep in a straight line. At home I locked my bike and started up the steps. By the time I got inside and changed out of my sweaty clothes I had decided to call Ash. He answered on the first ring.

"I need to talk to you," I said. "It's about Danielle's murder. I think it's important."

"I can come by in an hour, will that work?"

"Okay," I said. "I'll be at home."

I thought about what Sally had said. It was true Danielle went out of her way to piss off her mom. The drugs, the stripping, the temper tantrums. She knew exactly what would embarrass Sally, what would upset her, make her feel powerless, and that's what she did. I understood why, but even so, I felt sorry for Sally. She tried to believe she did the best she could, automatically justifying each of her mistakes. She knew how to spend money on a problem, and if that didn't work, she was lost.

And Danielle did not forgive. She was not someone you could fuck with. But that wasn't right, though, not exactly—people did fuck with Danielle, people hurt her all her life. Her uncle. Sally. Even her dad just left and never stayed in touch, never supported her. And then she got killed. How could someone do that to Danielle, when she was so tough and smart?

While I waited for Ash I called Sally back. She answered right away.

"Charlotte, honey," she said. "I'm so sorry—"

"I have a question," I said, cutting her off. "Where is your brother now?"

"I'm not sure. He's still in Denver, as far as I know. I haven't spoken to him since that Thanksgiving."

"Thanks," I said, and hung up.

I sat on the stoop, thinking and chain-smoking. If Danielle's two-point share of the development was three hundred thousand dollars, that meant the whole project was worth fifty times that amount. I did the calculation: fifteen million. It was crazy to think Danielle stood at the hinge of a deal that huge.

Finally Ash showed up.

"Hi," I said.

He sat down on the step beside me. "Charlotte, what's going on?"

"I saw Sally," I said.

"Sally Reeves?"

"She did something. Maybe something bad."

"Why do you think that?" Ash said.

"The land, because of the land."

"In Tomball? The inheritance?"

"Danielle wouldn't sell it, so now that she's dead Sally gets the land and she'll make a ton of money. She always hated Danielle. She pretended not to but she always did. Do you know how much money it is? Fifteen million dollars, and it all depended on her doing what Sally wanted. And Danielle wouldn't."

"Sally wasn't there," Ash said gently. "She was at home. We have phone records, alarm records, a browser history. She took calls, she couldn't have left without resetting the alarm."

"Maybe she got someone else to do it," I said. "Paid someone."

"We know about the land, about the development. We know all about it."

"Then do something."

"We're checking it out. Her financial records, her recent contacts. We are investigating it very carefully."

"Good," I said. "There's something else. Sally has a brother."

I told Ash about the abuse, the Thanksgiving dinner, and the rift between Sally and Danielle. "Maybe he came back," I said. "Maybe he hurt her. That's a motive, right? If she threatened to go to the police or something."

"Yeah," Ash said. "What's his name?"

"I don't know. Neither one of them ever said it."

"What else do you know about him?"

"He used to send Danielle birthday cards every year, in high school. That's it."

"Why didn't you tell me this before?"

"I'm sorry," I said. "I never told anyone. It was her secret."

"You have to be up front with me," he said. "If you're not honest, I won't be able to find out who killed her. You have to tell me everything."

I nodded, and without warning I began to sob. He sat next to me, his arm around my shoulders, waiting until I got my breath.

"What do you say we go inside?"

I stood and opened the door. My legs felt wobbly. Ash led me to the couch and brought me a glass of water.

"I need to ask you some more questions," he said. "You okay with that?"

I nodded.

"You ever hear about a guy named Eddie?" he said.

"No, who's that?" I said.

"Danielle didn't talk about him?"

I shook my head.

Ash frowned. "The clerk at the motel knew her. She worked out of there as an escort."

"She'd been to that place before?"

"A few times. She met at least one guy there. We have a description." Ash flipped a few pages of his notepad. "Medium height, five foot ten, white guy, late forties, dark hair, athletic."

"He was there that night?"

"No one saw him. He was there with Danielle two months ago. The guy who works there remembered them."

"Everybody remembers Danielle," I said.

"We have another statement that Danielle occasionally saw a john named Eddie. Might be this guy, might not."

"Who told you that?"

"Friend of Danielle's. Audrey Wright."

Why hadn't Audrey told me about that, I wondered. No one told me shit. Whatever happened, I was on the outside of it.

"Seems weird, though," I said. "That she would go there."

"Why?"

"That motel looked so crappy. I guess I thought she'd be more . . . expensive."

"You never know what people are into," he said. "Or where they go to hide."

"I guess," I said.

"So you didn't know about Eddie. What about Brandon Young, Danielle's boyfriend?"

"He wasn't really her boyfriend," I said.

"Okay, what was he?"

"A friend, you know, a good friend."

"They were sleeping together."

"Yeah. But it wasn't serious. He was trying to look out for her."

"Oh? How?"

"He gave her advice, but she didn't listen to him. He said it was the only time they ever got in a fight."

"When was this?"

Fuck, I thought. Ash didn't know. Brandon hadn't told him.

"Nothing, I mean, Danielle was really stubborn, it wasn't—"

"Where are you getting this information?"

"Brandon told me," I said. "Look, he's a good guy—"

"Charlotte. Tell me about the fight."

I started to cry again. This time Ash was impatient. He didn't try to comfort me.

"He's got a history of aggression," Ash said. "He was sleeping with the victim. And he has no alibi. If you have information I need to know it."

"It's not him," I said. "No way."

"Why no way? Because you like him? How well do you know him?"

"I just met him, at the memorial service."

"Charlotte, you need to be careful around these people. What if he did it? You want to protect a murderer?"

I thought about last night, the connection I'd felt with Brandon. Not the sex, but the way he talked to me . . . there was no way it could be him. I couldn't believe it.

"He wouldn't have hurt her," I said.

"Charlotte, what if you're wrong? Look, you don't have a choice. Tell me about the fight."

"This is not why I called you."

"You called because you want to help. Right?"

"Yeah."

"All right, tell me what he told you. It's not your job to protect him. All you have to do is tell me the truth. Tell me what you know. It's simple."

I was too confused and exhausted to resist anymore. I relayed the gist of my conversation with Brandon. I had to admit it looked bad for him. But I couldn't believe Sally wasn't involved in some way. If Danielle was that mad at Brandon for suggesting she sell the land, there was no way she would simply change her mind with Sally. I pointed this out and Ash nodded, taking notes.

"Please don't tell Brandon I told you all this," I said.

"Don't worry about that," he said. "I won't. You're doing the right thing."

"Whatever," I muttered, feeling utterly miserable. I lit another cigarette and watched him drive away. My throat was sore from smoking.

I went inside and poured a glass of whiskey, angry at myself for calling Ash, for betraying Brandon. And Sally, too, for that matter. I was crying again. I poured more whiskey. I thought of what Brandon had said: "Since Danielle died, I can't be sober."

On the wall hung a paint-by-number of egrets on a lake. My mom had bought it at a thrift store when I was a kid. The boundary of each shape had the same wildly trembling line. I drank and stared at it until the wobbly edges took over. I was retreating to the place where everything gets quiet and still, and I didn't have to think about Ash or Danielle or Sally or Brandon or my own fucking feelings. I practiced not breathing until I felt like nobody, like open space. I kept drinking, kept looking out the window. The sunset began in ugly pink streaks.

CHAPTER ELEVEN

The sunset faded and I turned on a lamp. I sat on the floor, flipping through an old *Southern Living* I'd brought home from the café. I studied a recipe for pressed herb pasta, thin sheets of dough encasing the tiniest leaves of basil and thyme, like flowers flattened in a book. I didn't have a pasta machine or know where to buy those baby herbs. Maybe you had to grow them? And if I made the recipe, what would I do, eat it? Have a dinner party? I marveled that such a thing existed in the world. It was so pretty and foreign and ridiculous I almost laughed.

My phone rang. It was Audrey.

"Hey," she said. "Are you busy tonight?"

"No."

"Can I come over?" she said. "I have weed."

"Sure," I said. "That sounds good."

A half hour later she sat in the chair by the window and pulled a one-hitter from her bag. It was painted to look like a cigarette, white with a brown filter. I poured her a drink and we smoked the weed.

"I can't stop thinking about Danielle," Audrey said.

"Me either."

Audrey passed the fake cigarette to me.

She said, "When we first met I knew she would be my best friend. I knew immediately."

"How?"

"We connected. It was like we already knew each other. I can't explain it."

"We became friends right away, too," I said. "I thought she was cool. I couldn't believe she liked me."

"How could she not?"

I shrugged. "She was rich, popular. I wasn't."

"Well, you're really easy to talk to. That matters more than money, you know?"

"I guess," I said. "She did need somebody to talk to. With all the shit that happened to her."

"What do you mean?"

"You knew, right?" I said. "That she was abused."

Audrey shrugged. "Yeah, that. Well, who wasn't?"

"Me," I said.

"I bet you were and you don't remember. People block it out. You have to get hypnotized and stuff."

"I don't think so," I said.

"Well, if you don't remember, that's what you would say."

"You're nuts."

"Whatever, I'm not the one with repressed memories."

"How do you know?" I said.

She giggled, and I did, too. I was glad to be high, to laugh and not be alone.

Audrey said, "I keep thinking about before she died. I stopped by Brandon's to borrow this top from Dani, this little blue silk halter with cutouts along the bottom, super cute, and we smoked weed and watched some reality show on TV, I can't even remember what show it was. And I left. With the fucking top. I should've stayed."

"Audrey, you were friends. You cared about her. Think about that part."

"I'm sick of being sad," she said. "I'm fucking tired from it."

"Me, too," I said.

She breathed out, as though to expel the sorrow. "Let's go out," she said. "It's a nice night."

"Sure."

I sat on my bed and watched Audrey hunt in my closet. She held a pink sequined party dress from the sixties I'd bought thrift shopping and never worn.

"Here we go. This is perfect," she said.

"You're wearing that?" I said.

"What size shoes are these?" She held a pair of sandals with rhinestone buckles.

"Eight," I said.

"They're a little big," she said. "But it'll do."

The sequins on the dress tossed light around the room as Audrey pulled it over her head. The pot made me slow, distracted by sensation. I sipped from my glass and had to close my eyes at the taste of the bourbon and the way it burned my throat.

"Hurry up, get ready," Audrey said.

She was talking from the bathroom, applying her makeup, and her tone altered as she stretched her face this way and that. I changed into a skirt and top and some pink wedges. I sat on the rim of the tub while she did my face. It tickled. I liked the sensation of her hands on my skin, her scrutiny and care. I smiled.

"Hold still," Audrey said, concerned with my eyeliner. She finished and I studied my face in the mirror. I looked like someone else. The makeup made my eyes smoky, glamorous.

I pocketed my keys and we went down the steps together. On my block there were no curbs, and trash accumulated in the muddy ditch. I kicked a lone brown shoe out of the way. Wrappers and bones from the chicken place were piled here and there. A scruffy dog lay in the shade across the street, gnawing on something.

"Chicken bones are bad for dogs," Audrey said. "They splinter."

"He does all right," I said. "His name is Tupac."

"That's awesome," she said. "Hop in."

We took 288 to 45 and got stuck in construction traffic for nearly an hour. Workers operated their machines under floodlights, and the jackhammer got into my head like grit. Her AC didn't work when the car was stopped, and we had to have the windows up to keep out the dust and noise. My clothes wrinkled and my enthusiasm flagged.

"Typical Houston," she said. "Sitting in traffic forever on our way to find drugs."

"It is emblematic," I said.

We got to a shithole bar on the north side. It smelled of stale cigarettes and cleaning products. Behind the bar were bottles of flavored vodkas, cheap gin, Southern Comfort.

"Don't worry," Audrey said. "This'll only take a second."

She went in a back room. I ordered a drink from a pale man with dyed black hair and inscrutable tattoos covering his skinny arms. He poured the drink in a plastic cup. Rust stains marked the sink behind him. After a minute he went to a shelf at the end of the bar and fiddled with an iPod until a ska song from the nineties blossomed from the speakers. He raised the volume and the bass rattled the bottles. Audrey came out, sniffing and shaking her head like a frightened horse.

"Let's get the fuck out of here," she said.

She had to yell over the music. I swallowed the drink. I was down from the pot by now, hungry, my brain swaddled in cold leather.

In the car, I said, "How about some food. Aren't we near those dim sum places?"

"Have a bump," Audrey said. "It'll clear your head."

I pinched some of the powder and breathed it off my palm. Immediately I felt focused, alert, *ready*. My throat tasted like detergent.

"Give me some," Audrey said. She snorted the coke and put the car in gear.

"Still hungry?" she asked.

"No."

"Good."

We drove to a bar called Slush and took over a picnic table. I ordered a martini with cucumber in it and Audrey got this slushy drink with rum, pink and fruity and cold. She slurped it through a straw. We sat under an umbrella adorned with logos of Mexican beer and a network of Christmas lights.

"This is what's so great about this town," she said.

"What?" I said.

"Well, you drive around all night, sweating in traffic."

"Yep," I said. "That's awesome."

"No, by the time you finally sit down with a drink, it's like you appreciate it more, because you earned it."

"Wow," I said, smiling. "Where does this optimism come from?"

"Necessity," she said gravely. She held her daiquiri aloft. "To Houston."

"To Houston," I agreed.

"You always lived here?" she said.

"My whole life."

"Your family, too?"

"It was just me and my mom," I said. "She died."

"I don't have family either," she said. "Sometimes I wonder what it would be like."

"I bet it's not always that great," I said. "Look at Danielle and Sally."

"Good point."

"I've been wondering if Sally had something to do with it. The timing of it. The money involved."

"They always say that in TV shows, the family members are the most likely suspects," Audrey said.

"It kind of freaks me out. I mean, I know Sally. I practically lived at her house."

"After your mom died?"

"No. Before."

The waitress came by and we ordered more drinks. We took long sips.

Audrey said, "I have a dead mom, too."

The way she said it, so casually, struck me as funny and I laughed without meaning to.

"What?" she said.

"I'm sorry. You make it seem like such a normal thing to have, when you put it that way: I have an apartment, I have a cheese sandwich. I have a dead mom."

"Yeah," she said. "I have a pair of scissors, an accordion, a Dolce handbag."

"Why do you have an accordion?"

"I found it in my place when I moved in," she said. "What, you don't?"

"No," I said, "but I have a CIA coffee mug that I found in my apartment."

"Close enough."

"It was weird. It was on the floor of the bedroom closet."

"That's where spies always keep their dishes."

"What happened, with your mom?" I said.

"It was years ago. She had cancer. How did yours die?"

"OD'd," I said. "Prescriptions."

"That sucks."

"It's weird," I said. "It's not like she took care of me. And it's not because I miss her. I mean, I miss her, sure. But that's not what bothers me. It's like now there's no buffer between me and . . . I guess everything."

Audrey nodded. "Exactly," she said. "You're alone."

"You're alone," I said. "And you're going to die."

Our little encampment under the umbrella seemed haunted. Danielle huddled in on one side, my mom on the other.

"It's like you're next," Audrey said.

"Yeah, as if it goes in order. Stupid to think that way."

"It's not stupid. I mean it feels true, right? But you don't have to be scared of it. It can make you free."

"What do you mean?" I asked.

"If you're going to die no matter what, you can do whatever you want. Nothing matters."

I wished I could believe that; it would make things easier.

"Nothing matters? Do you really think that?" I said. "There's nothing you care about?"

"That's not what I'm saying. I'm saying you can do anything you want."

"So what do you want to do?"

"I don't know. More blow."

She took my arm and we walked through the bar into the alcove of restrooms. Audrey pulled me into a stall and brought out the coke. With one more bump the world drifted from the stream of regular existence. I loved the separateness of it. I opened the stall door. Black granite covered the floor, the walls, the counter of sinks. The polished surface reflected light but the darkness underneath sucked it in. I watched the struggle between the stone and its sheen, like a tug-of-war, pulsating. I smelled the cocaine in my nostrils, a plastic bitterness that repulsed me if I gave it any thought. Back at the picnic table I was jittery, excited. The music played louder. We had to be close in order to hear.

"I saw one of your movies," I said. I heard my voice shaking.

"You did? Which one?"

Haltingly, I described the video of Danielle and Audrey together.

"Well?" she said. "What'd you think?"

Her words brushed against my face. They smelled like rum and mangoes. I hesitated. I didn't know how to talk about it, what I was supposed to say. A thread from my skirt was coming loose. I pulled at it.

"Quit," she said, her hand on mine. "You'll tear out the hem. We can cut it later."

She smoothed the skirt over my knee and squeezed my thigh.

"I loved that dress you wore," I said.

"Oh, I loved that dress, too," she said. "Fucking George ripped it during the shoot."

"I liked the beginning," I said. "The part where you're on that couch."

"Do you like girls?" she said.

"Um," I said.

My face flushed. I fished out the cucumber in my drink and nibbled it.

"People think I'm a dyke," she said.

"Are you?"

She made some gesture I couldn't decipher, perhaps a simple nerve response to the coke.

"I thought you were sexy," I said. "You looked—real."

"Thank you."

"But I'm not," I said.

"Not real?"

"I'm not gay," I said.

"Duh, Charlotte. Obviously. No one would ever, ever, ever mistake you for a lesbo."

Absurdly, I felt hurt. "Why not?" I said.

"Because, come on!"

"What?"

"You're such a fucking girl," she said.

"What do you mean?"

"I mean, like, here's how you stand, here's how you move your hands, you wear this frilly dress." She touched her pink party dress.

"Audrey, technically you are wearing that dress."

"So? It's your dress!"

"Still," I said, giggling.

"We're alike, us two," she said. "We have a lot in common."

I didn't see it, but I wished I could be more like Audrey, with her allure and easy laugh. She adjusted my skirt on my knee again, and kept her hand there.

"I was in love with her," she said.

"Who?"

"Danielle. Weren't you?"

"We were best friends," I said. "It was more like I wanted to *be* her."

"Do you think she loved me?" Audrey said. "She told me she did. But did she, really?"

"If she said she did, she probably did," I said.

"We never messed around except on camera. I don't know what it meant to her. I won't ever know."

"I'm sorry," I said.

"Ugh, anyway," she said. "We're not being sad tonight. Let's get another round."

We signaled the waitress. We drank. We snorted more coke. It helped.

"So you liked it," she said.

"What?"

"The video. You liked watching me?"

I nodded. She tucked my hair behind my ear. I felt hollow, deliciously empty, like a bubble that grows when you blow into it. Her fingers skimmed my neck and clavicle, making me shiver.

She took a handful of my hair and drew me towards her. She kissed me, opened my lips with hers. The emptiness inside me blossomed and blossomed until I didn't think I was there at all. Audrey touched my arm, my waist, my knee, her delicate fingers alighting, leaving each place aglow with nerves. I quit thinking about Danielle and Sally and Brandon and my mom. She kissed me again and her desire rolled through me, like the opposite of fear. I was dissolving inside her smallness, her softness. I had no idea what might happen next, and not knowing thrilled me.

Audrey giggled. "Check them out," she said, pointing.

On the picnic bench near us a couple of guys sat watching. I accidentally made eye contact with one. I didn't care. Their attention confirmed this was actually happening.

Audrey said, "Fuck this. Let's go." We walked out to the parking lot, Audrey leading, tugging on my hand. In the car I sat awkwardly. The people at the bar had made me feel safe, like we were in a clearing in the woods, protected by trees. Being alone with her, each move required deliberation. She parked on the street outside my apartment and we went upstairs and inside.

"Want something to drink?" I said, opening the fridge.

"No. Come here."

"Okay." I shut the refrigerator door.

"I like hanging out with you," she said.

"Me, too," I said. I blushed.

She stepped towards me, more tentative than before, and we kissed. Strange to touch a girl. Her soft mouth, the fineness of her skin disoriented me. My hands were clumsy, oversized on her tiny shoulders. I leaned against the doorframe. She touched my face, my breasts. She pulled my shirt over my head, her eyes wide, observing. My nipples hardened at her touch, and my thighs tensed. She gasped as my body jerked. I unzipped her dress and lowered the loose top off her shoulders, revealing her tits, the long brown nipples I had seen on the video.

She yanked my skirt up around my hips, roughly. She pushed my thong to the side, slid her finger inside me. I cried out. The emptiness converged around her hand. I wanted more, I wanted more. She stopped and I thought I might sob.

I reached for her. She grabbed my wrists, kissed me on the mouth and down my neck. She kissed my breasts and licked them, her tongue darting out and in, sliding over my skin, warming it and leaving it wet and cool. Her grip on my wrists stayed firm. It made me less nervous, not having to do anything with my hands.

"Please," I said, barely able to speak.

"Please what," she said, but I didn't know what to say.

I loved her mouth on my body. I loved her topless, seeing her nipples get hard.

"Take off your clothes," she said.

I wiggled out of them, embarrassed at how wet I was.

Strands of it fell down my thighs. I ran my fingers over her tits, the nipples against my palms. I took one in my mouth. She stood still and her breath came quicker. I liked hearing it. She stepped out of her panties. She was hairless there, slick and pink and swollen. I glanced at her face, met her eyes, looked away. She pressed my head to her chest and pushed me down.

I knelt, her hands on my head, and kissed her. She tasted like lemons, like wine about to turn. She was whispering nonsense syllables, high-pitched sighs that came from her throat. She pushed into me now, grinding. Her voice grew louder, wavered in conjunction with her body. She wouldn't hold still. Suddenly, I had to make her hold still. It was a feeling foreign to me, akin to fury. I fucked her with my hand, faster. I wanted to bite her, but I didn't. She gave a staccato cry, and her whole body stiffened, her muscles pulsed. She stopped moving and rested against the wall. I was amazed I could bring such a thing about.

My knees hurt from kneeling. I wiped my face on my arm and stood. Audrey slumped, whimpering, her eyes glazed. I kissed her mouth and she jumped at my touch before melting into me. She moved her hand from my waist over my belly, down. She studied me with a vacant expression, open-eyed. I moved against her palm, involuntary. She stared hard at my face as though from a distance.

She shoved her fingers in roughly. It hurt, maybe, though my body was confused and didn't care. She kissed me and I didn't have to think. My mind switched off and I let it. Audrey was controlling my heartbeat, my breath, making me shake. My body gave up trying to understand what it felt. I yelled as I came, and clung to her, not believing my own sounds.

"Come on," she said. "Lie down."

I took a few trembling steps to the bed and collapsed. My

confusion dissolved in her tender kisses and she touched me, softly, until I bucked against her again. My heart rate slowed and my will returned. She left and came back and I understood I had been asleep, for how long I had no idea. She knelt by the bed, slender and naked. I hoped she would lie down with me and then I didn't. I wished a man was there, someone strong to hold me. I said her name.

"You're not like her, are you?" she said. "You like it, even with no one watching."

Her voice sounded sad. I didn't know how to answer. She smiled and touched my face and we slept.

CHAPTER TWELVE

I woke and extracted myself from Audrey's arms. The bright day chiseled at my head. I felt poisoned. I got in the shower and stood under the water until it ran cold, then dressed in jeans and a blue cowboy shirt with white birds embroidered above the pockets. My skin felt sensitive. I moved carefully around the apartment, brewed a pot of coffee, gathered up last night's clothes from the middle of the living room floor. I was pulling on my boots when Audrey awoke.

"Hey," she said.

"Hey."

She sat up and rubbed her eyes. Her beauty seemed magnified in the morning light, her makeup smeared, her hair disheveled. I didn't know what to say to her. I felt impaired, awkward.

"Do you want some coffee?" I said. "Or a shower? You can take a shower if you want. I'm going out for cigarettes."

"Okay," she said.

"Make yourself at home. I'll be back in a few minutes."

I slid sunglasses on and walked to the gas station five blocks away. There was a closer store, but I needed the time away, and the space. I'd never been with a girl before, not like that. I didn't know what it meant or how to act. I wondered what she was thinking. Everything felt out of context. There were no boundaries anywhere. My regular life, work and running and hanging out with Michael, had gotten so far away. None of it was possible now.

I smoked on the way home, taking my time. The cigarette made me feel dirty. Upstairs I was relieved to find Audrey was in the shower. I sipped coffee. The caffeine only reactivated the coke, agitating me.

Audrey came out of the bathroom wrapped in a towel, an opened beer in her hand.

"Found it in the fridge," she said. "I love drinking beer in the shower. I felt like shit when I first woke up, did you?"

"I'm still a little shaky," I said.

"Here," she said, handing me the beer, still half full. "This will help. Can I borrow some clean clothes?"

"Sure," I said. "Whatever you want."

After a few sips of beer I started to relax and my headache eased up. Audrey emerged from my closet in a yellow sundress, and it gave me a feeling of déjà vu. Something about drinking in the morning, the way the light came in the window.

"Danielle used to always borrow my clothes," I said.

"Yeah, mine, too. She was like a poacher. Of tank tops."

"She used to live here, you know."

"What?" Audrey said. "In this apartment?"

"Yeah. A couple of years ago. Before prison and all that."

Audrey looked around in wonder. "How long have you lived here?" she said.

"Since middle school. It was my mom's place. I inherited the lease."

"I've never lived anywhere a whole year," she said. "Don't you get tired of it?"

"I don't know. I don't think about it. There was never a reason to move, you know?"

"The memories don't bother you?"

"Wouldn't I still have memories if I moved? I'd have the same brain."

"No, you get a new brain when you sign a lease," she said. "I can't believe you didn't know that."

"In that case I should definitely move. Not all the memories are bad, though."

"I hate to think about the past," Audrey said, finishing the beer. "Even good memories make me sad. 'Cause they're over."

"I see what you mean."

"Do you want to go get breakfast?" She picked up a pink barrette of mine and stuck it in her hair.

"I don't think I can eat," I said. "Not yet."

"Poor baby, still feeling bad? I guess we drank a lot."

"And the coke," I said. "I'm not used to it."

"I had fun last night, though," Audrey said. She smiled at me. "Let's split another beer."

"Okay." I got a beer from the fridge and lit a cigarette while she loaded her one-hitter.

"This will make you feel better, too," she said, handing it to me.

I took a hit and held it, watching her in the yellow dress. My apartment felt less stable with her in it. Less like mine. She reminded me too much of Danielle. It was unsettling.

"That dress looks awesome on you," I said. "You should keep it."

"Don't be silly, I'll give it back. I like wearing your clothes, though."

"Really, why?"

"I don't know. They're cute. They smell like you."

"Fabric softener."

"Is that what it is? I like it."

"It's pretty attainable. I buy it at the grocery store."

She laughed, leaned over, kissed me on the mouth. Again I was shocked by her softness and her delicate lips. Electric flashes from the previous night shot through my body. I recoiled, my head spinning.

"Sorry," I said. "I feel sick."

"Okay, I'll go. Call me later, okay?"

I let her out the front door. It was a relief to be alone and have some time to think, to get organized. I drank a glass of water, ate a piece of toast, and took my clothes to the Laundromat. I sat on top of a washer while a handful of Mexican kids played and shrieked around me. Every few minutes they would assemble to work out some new rules to their game, which involved jumping out from behind the machines and growling like lions. A girl my age called out to a little boy. She gave him a cup of applesauce and he sat on the floor to eat it. She folded a sheet into a sharp square and picked up another. I wished I could fold myself up that neatly.

I thought about Audrey. She was so good at distracting herself from Danielle. I didn't understand how she did it. The drugs helped, obviously. Sex and drugs. But still, I couldn't get Danielle out of my head. I couldn't stop wondering who killed her, or thinking about those pictures of her, or the videos. It was all jumbled up in my head, along with what Detective Ash had suggested that night at House of Pies—that maybe I had something to do with it. It didn't make sense, but it kept nagging at me. I transferred my clothes to the dryer and called him.

He answered on the second ring.

"Hey, it's Charlotte," I said.

"Yeah," he said. "What can I do for you?"

"I just wondered if you found anything out. About Sally? Or her brother?"

"Yeah, we did. I was meaning to call you. We checked up on him. We found out this morning, the uncle's out of the picture."

"Are you sure?" I said.

"Positive. He's been in prison for three years. Good alibi."

"For what?" I said.

"For rape," he said. "He was doing it out there. In Colorado. They finally caught him."

"Oh my god," I said.

"So it's not him. And he won't hurt any more little girls. He'll be locked up a long time."

"What about Sally?"

"I told you before, we've been very thorough, we haven't found anything that leads us in that direction."

"But it's so much money, and they always fought. And the timing of it—"

"Charlotte, right now you need to just sit tight. Be patient. We will be making an arrest fairly soon, I think."

"Who?"

"I can't talk about it. But be careful. Steer clear of Brandon Young."

"You think it was him."

"I'll let you know when we have something definitive." He hung up.

Back home I put my clean clothes away. I began to tidy my shoes, lining them in pairs on the floor of the closet. The corners of the closet were dusty, so I got the broom and dustpan, and then the trash needed taking out, and I spilled coffee grounds on my shirt. I took it off to try to wash it in the sink and I tripped over a pile of shoes I had moved in order to sweep, and banged my knee against the bed. "Motherfucker," I said aloud. I kicked the shoes into a corner, the shirt with it, and started to cry.

If I had said something years ago, when I first found out about Danielle's uncle, if I had convinced her to go to the police, then maybe he would have been in prison a long time ago. I never thought about it at the time. But I should have. How many girls had he hurt in Colorado?

I put on running clothes and went out in the heat of the day. I circled the zoo and the fountain, feeling the toxins sweating out of my body. I was punishing myself. I ran alongside the art museum. Its cool stone rose from the sidewalk, making me feel small and ephemeral. Usually it was a nice contrast from everything that was cheap and new, from brainless nights of television, takeout dinners from the strip mall, the irritating whine of mosquitoes. But today I didn't find it comforting. I wondered if Danielle had even known her uncle was in prison, and if she did, how she felt about it. She and Audrey both were good at making light of serious things. Maybe that's why they liked each other so much. They could just do drugs and hang out, gliding along the surface.

I never got addicted to drugs when Danielle did. After a couple of days of being high, I wanted a break. I craved order, time alone, exercise. Danielle just wanted more pills. I knew it wasn't any kind of strength of character. I wasn't better than her. We both did whatever we felt like. It was only luck that what I wanted was not as dangerous. I used to think she was the lucky one, with her rich mom, her fancy house, her beauty and popularity. Things looked different now. Poor Danielle. The thing with her uncle, getting addicted to dope, even getting caught, all of that was bad luck. There were plenty of illegal things I had done, but I never went to prison. And now the murder. It was like she was cursed.

I slowed to a walk for the last half mile, breathing hard, feeling weak and thirsty and sad, but calmer. Until I saw Michael sitting on my steps. An iced coffee sweated in his hand. He was wearing sunglasses. I couldn't see his eyes.

"Hey," he said.

"What the fuck are you doing here?" I said.

"I wanted to talk to you."

"You could have called."

"I didn't think you would answer the phone," he said.

He was right, I wouldn't have. I shrugged, stepped past him, and unlocked the door. He followed me inside. In the kitchen I drank a glass of water and filled it again from the tap. I splashed water on my face.

"So, you're here. What do you want?" I said.

"I missed you," he said. "I wanted to apologize for the way I've handled things."

"What things? You mean cheating on me? And dumping me? To go back with the girl you said was too self-involved to be in a relationship. Too immature. Y'all had nothing in common. That's what you told me."

"I'm sorry, really I am. You're great. I love you. I wish this had never happened."

"Tired of her already?" I said.

"It's not that."

"Does she know you're here?"

"Actually, no."

"Huh. Interesting."

"Charlotte, I realize you're mad. You have a right to be."

"I'm not mad," I said. I tried to call up my feelings when he'd first told me about her, and when I saw them together. I had been hurt, and yes, angry. It was only last week but it seemed so long ago. I didn't feel much now. Sad, maybe.

He picked up a bracelet from the coffee table and played with it, spinning it around his finger. It was Audrey's, she must have left it. I had such a hard time imagining the two of them, Michael and Audrey, occupying the same world. I wondered what he'd think of me if I told him about her. About me and her. I blushed. Suddenly I couldn't stand him being in my apartment.

"Put that down," I said. "Let's go outside."

We wandered down the block and turned on Binz, retracing my jogging route. It was a relief to see him, in a way. He was familiar, even if he was an asshole. He was part of my regular life, before all this Danielle shit. I felt almost normal.

We went on, past the corner store and the chicken place and the Jamaican restaurant, and gradually the cracked sidewalks gave way to newer pavement. Landscaped shrubs and lawns replaced the patchy grass and garbage. On the next block lights illuminated the children's museum's bright cartoon caryatids. I lit a cigarette.

"Look, I made a mistake," he said. "It's not working out with her."

"That was quick. Hardly worth all this drama, really."

"I know," he said.

"Is she still too immature for you? Or maybe you liked fucking her in secret. It's not fun now she's your actual girlfriend?"

"It's not that. It's you. I can't stop thinking about you. The other night at the bar, seeing you—"

"Look, I'm sorry about that," I said. "I wasn't at my best." I didn't tell him the rest, getting pulled over, all that. It seemed so long ago.

"It was my fault," Michael said. "We shouldn't have gone there."

"Why not?"

"I knew it was your favorite place. I guess we should have discussed it ahead of time, to avoid running into each other."

"Bar custody?" I said. "Jesus, that's sad."

"Well, it's too small a town. We should have talked it over."

"There's six million people here," I said.

"You know what I mean."

"Yeah."

"I hate that I hurt you," he said. I could tell he meant it.

"It's okay," I said. "I'm over it."

"What's going on with you?" Michael said.

"What do you mean?"

"I guess I thought you'd be more upset with me. At least a little more."

"A lot's happened," I said.

"You met somebody."

"That's actually none of your business, at this point."

"Seriously? Already? Not that idiot you were with at the bar?"

"Michael, stop it."

"It is him. That guy? Fuck."

"No, it's not. It's not what you think, okay? Danielle, my old friend, remember her?"

"The stripper? What about her?"

"She died. Compared to that, I kind of don't give a fuck about you and your little girlfriend, or who you're fucking, or whatever."

"Oh my god, Charlotte, I had no idea."

"Yeah, well."

"I'm sorry."

"She was murdered," I said. "I've had to talk to the cops. I've visited her mother. I went to the memorial service. At a fucking church. That's what I've been up to while you've been fucking around with your ex-girlfriend."

I turned around and walked back the way we came. He trotted behind me to catch up.

"Michael, I'm going home," I said.

"Okay."

"I don't want you to come with me."

"Charlotte, if I'd known you were dealing with all this—"

"Then what? You wouldn't have told me about what's-her-name?"

"No, I—"

"You would have kept lying to me a little longer?"

"Charlotte, I care about you. I love you. I want to be your friend, I can be here for you, will you stop?"

I was walking so fast I might as well have been running. He was sweating through his T-shirt. He reached out to grab my shoulder. I stopped and closed my eyes, trying not to cry. He stepped close and hugged me. I felt crushed, not from the pressure of his embrace, but some other force. It was like my chest imploded and my arms hung loose from an empty frame. We stood together, breathing, on the street in front of the muddy ditch.

"Charlotte, I'm sorry," he whispered into my hair.

"I know," I said.

"Let me walk you home."

"No. It's too late," I said. "Or too soon, or something."

He nodded. "Will you be okay?"

"I'm fine," I said. "Don't worry about me."

I left him standing on the sidewalk. I passed the new townhomes with their Home Depot lanterns and then the dingy apartment complexes on my block. I went up the steps and inside. I thought about the mornings Michael used to stay over.

We'd sit on the couch facing each other, drinking coffee, and he would put his bare feet on top of my feet and we'd talk about what we had to go do that day. It was nice. He was pleasant to be around. Still, half the time I wished he'd leave so I could be alone. He didn't understand certain truths about life—its sadness. Its difficulty. He'd had a happy childhood. He didn't know the way I'd grown up. I never told him about it. No one knew, except my mom, and Danielle. Only dead people.

I felt worn out, thinking of all the people whose lives were suddenly intertwined with mine: Audrey, Brandon, Sally, Danielle. What did any of them have to do with me, really? I ought to try to get my job back. Or some job, anyway, maybe a different one. I vowed to do it tomorrow. Either call my boss or go fill out some applications. I got a beer from the fridge and watched some crappy TV, relieved to be by myself and not think.

CHAPTER THIRTEEN

I slept late the next day and woke up to my ringing phone. I answered when I saw Audrey's name on the caller ID.

"What are you doing?" she asked.

"Sleeping."

"Come with me to Brandon's. I'm worried about him."

"Why? What's wrong?"

"He's not answering his phone. He does that when he gets too depressed. Let's go cheer him up."

"I don't know," I said. I didn't feel too great about seeing Brandon. I kind of wanted a break from Audrey, too.

"Oh, come on. I'm right by your house, anyways."

"I was gonna go do some stuff. Look for a job."

"Well, I'm coming over. I'll be there in a few." She hung up.

It was after noon. I showered and drank coffee, made a peanut butter sandwich. I was eating it when she got there.

"Hey," she said at the top of the steps. "Let's smoke real quick."

She loaded a wooden pipe and lit it, handed it to me.

"I can't go," I said, taking the pipe.

"Oh, come on. You're not seriously going to look for a job right now, are you?"

"Sure," I said. "Maybe I shouldn't be smoking."

"Come on, I don't want to hang out with Brandon by myself, it's too depressing. All he does is cry and talk about Danielle. If you're there maybe he'll make more of an effort."

"The cops think he killed her," I said.

"Well, he didn't."

"Are you sure?"

"Yes, I'm fucking sure."

"But what if they're right?"

"Look, I know him. Do you think he did it? Can you picture it?"

"No. Not really."

"So what's your deal? Why are you being all sketchy? Just come with me."

I took another hit from the pipe and held it. I decided to tell her.

"I had sex with him," I said. "It was before you and me, you know . . . it only happened once. We did some ketamine and smoked and it just happened."

"He's such a slut," she said.

"You're not upset?"

"Whatever, I can tell you like me."

I smiled.

"I did K once," she said. "With him and Dani. I mean, Dani didn't do it, she only smoked weed. It freaked the fuck out of me. I couldn't move and the walls turned into trees with hands, and they couldn't move either. And we couldn't find each other. It was the worst."

"Trees with hands?"

"They went to grab me. We were paralyzed and couldn't get away. And they kept changing colors. I would not touch that shit again."

"Sounds horrible," I said.

"Please come help me cheer him up?"

"There's something else, too," I said.

Audrey refilled the pipe and hit it. "What?" she said around the smoke.

"I told the detective about him and Danielle fighting. I feel terrible about it."

"Jesus."

"That's bad, right?"

"I don't know. Maybe."

"Brandon doesn't know it was me, probably. I thought he'd already told them."

She thought for a minute. "Well, it happened. Their fight, I mean. You didn't lie."

"No."

"And you didn't mean to. You worry too much. Maybe we can take him to the movies. He loves movies."

"You really want me to go with you, huh?"

"Is it obvious?" She reached over and took hold of my hair, pulling me towards her. The kiss left me empty-headed and gasping.

"You're very persuasive," I said.

"Good. Let's go."

In the car I said, "Has that detective been talking to you, too? Ash?"

"He asked me a bunch of questions. Pain in the ass."

"Yeah, totally. What'd you tell him?"

"Nothing. I don't know what happened. He finally let me go."

"I hope he catches the guy," I said.

"Yeah."

"Can I ask you something? Do you think he's kind of hot?"

She looked at me like I was nuts. "He's a cop," she said.

"I know, but still."

"I can't believe you like him," she said.

"I don't like him. I think he's attractive, that's all."

"You have weird taste."

"All right, forget I said anything."

"I wonder if he's, like, into handcuffs and stuff like that. Like role-playing, uniforms."

"I don't get the whole uniform fetish," I said. "To me people always look uncomfortable in them."

"Once I had to dress up like a prison warden for a shoot," Audrey said. "It was so silly. I wore this khaki outfit with a badge on it, and platform heels."

"I wouldn't mind seeing that."

"Well, you can, it's on the fucking Internet. I carried this nightstick, too. But it was actually a dildo."

We dissolved into giggles.

She said, "I hope Brandon will be okay. He told me he's been calling in sick to work."

"Maybe that's good," I said. "He could probably use a break. To grieve, you know?"

"Yeah, no shit he could use a break. Have you seen the public-access channel?"

"No, I don't have cable."

"It's weird, it has these shows like 'My Skin Is on Fire: Living with Psoriasis.' I have it."

"You have psoriasis?"

"Ha ha," she said.

"What is psoriasis, anyway?" I asked.

"I think it's where your skin is on fire. If you had cable you would know this."

I smiled.

At Brandon's house we rang the bell. His car was in the drive, but he didn't answer the door.

"He's probably asleep," she said. "I know how to get in."

We went around to a screened porch in the back, cluttered with plastic furniture. A pot of dirt sat on a wicker table by the kitchen door. Audrey lifted it and retrieved a spare key, unlocked the door, and pushed it open to the kitchen. The air inside was stuffy and smelled like rotting garbage. I followed behind her, listening, trying to sense anyone in the house.

"Brandon, what the F?" Audrey called out. "Wake up!"

She lit a cigarette and opened the fridge, grabbed a can of Diet Coke. I walked past her into the dining room. A vintage movie poster on foam core was nailed to the yellow wall. Piles of mail littered the table, along with DVDs in paper envelopes. Through the archway I could see the living room and the front window. The smell was terrible.

The couch was missing a cushion. I saw the corner of it on the floor, behind the coffee table, on his Ikea rug with the oversized green and red floral design. Thin hardwood boards ran diagonally, like they made in the twenties. I was wondering, Could this house be that old? as I stepped around the table. Brandon lay on the floor, faceup, wedged between the couch and table, his body twisted. One arm was pinned under him.

"Audrey!" I yelled.

Bad sweetness bloomed off him, filling the room. Vomit had dried on his face and the rug. He wore shorts and scuffed white tennis shoes, with one lace partway undone. I tried to take a breath and retched, gripping the table for support. Bile burned my throat. I vomited on the floor. A chair lay on its side next to me. Had it been that way or had I knocked it over? I took a deep breath but there was no air, only the smell. His body filled my throat, my nose. I retched again and ran, bumping into Audrey.

"Outside," I gasped, grabbing her arm.

We stumbled through the yard and I leaned against the tree by the fence, far from the house. I squatted down, hunched over, hugged my knees. Audrey stood over me, trying to balance in the yard on her high heels.

"What?" she asked. "Charlotte, you're freaking me out."

I gulped air, forced my breath deep and even. The smell was not as strong out here. "He's dead," I said, when I could talk.

"No, he's not," she said. "Quit it. What's wrong with you?" She was backing away from me and turning towards the house.

"Audrey, don't go in there," I said. She ignored me. I watched her disappear through the kitchen door. She came out a minute later looking white, shaky.

"He's dead," she said.

"Yes. We need to call the cops," I said.

"I don't know," she said.

"Yes, that's what we do." I was thinking clearly then. "Let's go to the car. I'll call Ash, and you . . ." I thought for a minute. "Drugs," I said. "Weed, coke, whatever you have on you, in your car, you have to get rid of it. We'll hide it somewhere."

I stood, took her hand, and led her out of the yard and to the car. Audrey was like a doll whose limbs you had to manually move. She walked slowly alongside me, the cigarette forgotten between her fingers. She was so unresponsive. It was starting to scare me. "It's going to be okay," I told her, then repeated it.

Some kids were playing on swings at the park across the street, their tummies draped over the seats, arms and legs dangling in the grooves of dirt. I watched them, confused. How could they be there, in the same world as me and Audrey and everyone who was dead? I got hold of my phone and dialed.

"Ash," he answered.

"Charlotte," I said. "It's Charlotte Ford."

"Charlotte, what's wrong?"

"I'm at Brandon's house," I said.

"I told you to stay away from him."

"He's dead."

"Shit," he said. "I'm coming now. Stay where you are and talk to the officers when they arrive. Are you hurt?"

"No," I said.

"I'll be there soon as I can, okay?"

"Okay." I hung up.

"He's on his way," I said to Audrey.

She sat in the driver's seat, frozen, not responding.

"Audrey, where's the weed?" I said. "We have to hide it."

She didn't answer. Her eyes did not seem to focus.

"Come on," I said. "They'll be here soon."

Finally she looked at me.

"No," she said. "I don't want to see the cops."

"We have to."

"And tell them what?" she said. "We don't know anything."

"Audrey, we can't leave. I already called them."

"You stay if you want," she said. She closed the car door and put her seat belt on. "I'm sorry. I can't." She turned the key, shifted into drive, and pulled away.

I walked up and down the sidewalk in front of Brandon's house. Cars honked on Main, a few blocks down. The sidewalk slab buckled under an old bur oak and the roots showed through. The formation of roots made a contorted shape that resembled a dog. A squad car turned the corner and parked in front of the house. Two uniformed cops got out.

"Charlotte Ford?" one of them said.

I nodded.

"Tell me what happened," he said.

"Brandon's dead," I said. "I went in the kitchen door. It's unlocked."

"Wait here," the man said.

They walked around back. I leaned against the tree until they came out, and I answered their questions. What time had I arrived? Why was I there? When had I last seen Brandon, heard from him? What was the nature of our relationship, what had I touched inside the house? It went on and on. I didn't mention Audrey. I didn't want to get her in trouble.

Soon the street filled with vehicles. An ambulance pulled quietly behind the squad car. Ash parked his SUV and got out, nodded to me, and walked up Brandon's steps. Another squad car came. I sat on a bench across the street and smoked cigarette after cigarette, lining the butts on the sidewalk next to my foot. The light slanted into dusk on the bench. All the time I worried about Audrey.

Eventually Ash came outside and sat on the bench next to me.

"What are you doing here, Charlotte? I told you to steer clear."

"Well, he's not going to hurt anybody now, is he," I said.

He sighed. "Tell me what happened."

"I already told the other guy all of this."

"Now tell me," he said.

I went through it again, and as I described finding Brandon's body, it seemed unreal, like I was making it up. Why was I talking about any of this stuff, when we were right there in front of Brandon's house and I ought to go in and sit on the couch and him and me and Audrey could smoke a bowl and talk and go to the movies like we planned. It was so absurd to be out here on the bench instead that I started to laugh. But the laughter sounded wrong, like fucked-up coughing, and I stopped.

"I'm sorry," I said.

"For what?"

"I don't know."

I figured something must be my fault. Before I came into these people's lives they were fine, they were okay. I bit down, imagined my teeth cracking from the pressure. My thoughts were heavy objects falling from a great height. They hit the ground without bouncing; they sank and disappeared. I had a vision in which my eyes retreated deep into their sockets and vanished, and I never had to see again. I seemed to be crying.

Ash was talking. "Looks like he overdosed, Charlotte."

"Why did he do it? How did it happen?"

"They'll do tests. We found ketamine in the house. We see that sometimes, with club drugs. Especially injecting, it's hard to gauge the dose."

"Injecting? He used needles?"

"Apparently we're waiting on forensics. We'll find out more. When did you last talk to him?"

"A few days ago. Before I saw you last."

"How did he seem?"

"Sad. He was sad."

Ash nodded.

"I saw a dead person before," I said. "My mom. I found her, too."

"That's hard," he said. "I'm sorry."

The front door opened and the ambulance guys were bringing a stretcher through. It had Brandon on it, covered up. Ash went to talk to them and I was alone on the bench. After a few minutes, I walked down the street through the neighborhood, away from Brandon's house and his body and all the police cars. I passed tidy houses flickering with television. People washed dishes, their cats perched on their front steps, the coals in their grills burned themselves out. It was a toy world, unreal. On North Main the traffic streamed by in rivulets of light. I turned and walked past gas stations and closed shops until I found a bar.

I opened the door onto neon and stools, a glowing cigarette machine and a window unit diligently laboring. I ordered whiskey from the bartender, a frayed girl with sloping shoulders. I took the drink to a booth in the corner where the wrinkles in the leather seat looked like veins.

I called Audrey and left a message, then I called her again, then I sent her a text. I sipped my drink and listened to songs on the jukebox. I listened to them carefully, as though music was a source of information, divorced from aesthetics or pleasure. I finished my bourbon. I tried Audrey again and hung up when the voice mail answered. I asked the bartender for the number of a cab and smoked cigarettes outside while I waited for it. I sat on a bench in front of the bar, studying the dandelions and sparkles of broken glass at my feet.

On the way home I wondered if Brandon killed himself on purpose. Of course I'd wondered the same thing about my mom. I used to get so scared each time she went off her meds. Not of the violence, or the way she suffered through withdrawal, though that was horrible enough. The longer she stayed off meds, the higher the risk of overdose once she started again. I stayed vigilant, waking her from naps once an hour or so, to make sure she wasn't comatose. I called 911 more than once. The first time I was thirteen.

I called the last time one month after my eighteenth birthday. I didn't think she meant to do it, but I had to consider the timing. The social workers came around once, and I assured them I was fine. I was a legal adult. They couldn't send me to a foster home or some other horrific place. I finished out the school year, graduated with honors. Accident or not, I knew my mother loved me, because she waited until I turned eighteen. Sometimes, out of nowhere, I missed her like crazy.

At home I went upstairs and opened a beer. The phone rang.

"Charlotte, where are you?" Ash said. He sounded pissed off.

"I'm at home," I said.

"Are you all right? You just wandered off. I wasn't finished with you."

"Well," I said. "You can come here, I guess."

He said okay and hung up. A half hour later he knocked on my door.

"Listen, Charlotte. It's over. It was him."

"What was him?"

"Brandon Young. If he were alive, we would be charging him right now with Danielle's murder."

"I don't believe it," I said.

"You don't have to believe it for it to be true."

"Jesus," I said.

I sat down on the couch and Ash took a chair.

"Was it suicide?" I said.

Ash shrugged. "We didn't find a note. Could be."

I played with the label on my beer bottle, peeling it up at one corner.

"Do you have another one of those?" he asked me.

"Yeah, in the fridge."

"Thanks."

He got it and came and sat back down.

"Guess you're off duty?" I said.

"More or less. I'll finish up the paperwork over the next few days."

"It was true, what you said, wasn't it?"

"What?"

"Danielle's murder. It did have to do with me. You said I was the thing that was different in her life. The anomaly."

"Yeah?"

"If I hadn't told Danielle about the inheritance, she and Brandon would never have got in a fight about it, and they'd both still be alive."

"Charlotte, you can't think that way."

"Why not? It's true."

"You could just as easily blame Sally, or Danielle's great-aunt for dying of old age. The only person responsible for her death is Brandon Young. He killed her. Not anybody else. Not you."

I didn't say anything.

"What were you doing there, anyway? You could have been hurt."

"Audrey took me there," I said. "We were going to try and cheer him up." I hadn't mentioned her earlier, but what did it matter now? The investigation was over. The cops would leave her alone. "She just wanted me along for company," I said. "Because he was so depressed."

"She left you there?"

I nodded. "She saw him, too. His body. She freaked out."

"She was at the scene? Inside the house?"

"Yeah."

"And you didn't think to tell me this?"

"Sorry."

"Charlotte, these people, what are you doing with them?"

"You mean Audrey and Brandon?"

"Yeah. You didn't know them before, right? They were Danielle's friends, not yours. You don't belong with them."

"What's that supposed to mean?"

"One thing it means is if you find a dead body, the person you are with should not just leave you there. You deserve better than that."

"Oh, come on. He was her friend. I mean, I barely knew him, but she—"

"I'm just saying you deserve more."

He leaned forward, touched my knee. I looked up. His face was kind, concerned. The skin around his eyes was textured in tiny crisscrosses. I wanted to touch it. I wondered how old he was. Forty, maybe? Not too old.

"I know you loved Danielle, you grew up together, I understand that. But it seems to me like she made a lot of bad decisions. I wouldn't necessarily use her life as a template. There's better ways to pick your friends."

"Yeah? Like what?" I said, defensive.

"Like find people who are nice to you and help you and don't get you involved in their bullshit drama. And their drugs and all that."

"What makes you think I'm any different from them?" I said. "Or from Danielle?"

"Charlotte, I'm a detective, remember?" He grinned at me.

He was right, maybe, but what did he want? I couldn't figure him out. Besides, Audrey needed someone. She was fucked up, sure, but her two best friends had just died. I was worried about her even now, though I also had to admit I was glad she wasn't there. And Ash was.

"I'm gonna get another beer," I said. "Want one?"

"I should get going."

"Lecture's over?"

"For now." He smiled and squeezed my hand.

"Can I ask you something?" I said.

"Yeah."

"How long was he like that?"

"You mean when did he die? We don't know yet. We only have a rough estimate. A couple of days, probably. Why?"

"I just wondered."

"Try not to think about it. It's over."

"Yeah, right. How do I not think about it?"

He sat next to me and put his arm around me. "Sorry," he said. "I know it's not that easy. If you need someone to talk to about it, you can call me."

"Thanks," I said.

I breathed him in, warm skin and hair and faint sweat. We sat like that for a moment, and I thought if I could stay in his arms it might be possible to forget the smell of Brandon's body. To believe it was really over.

"Charlotte, once I've finished with the case, filed all the forms—like I said, it should take a few days. After that, say next week sometime, can I make you dinner?"

"You cook?" I said.

"I'm a great cook, actually."

"Like a date?"

"Yes, like a date."

"Isn't this kind of unprofessional?" I asked. But I could feel myself smiling.

"That's why I said next week. When the case is officially closed. Just say yes."

"Okay. You can cook me dinner."

"Good. I'll call you."

I walked him to the door and he took my hand again and

kissed me on the cheek. I watched him go down the steps and get in his car. He waved and drove away.

After he left I undressed for a hot bath. I tried to imagine what it would be like to date a cop. I gave up on that idea because it was too strange and thought instead about his lips against my cheek.

CHAPTER FOURTEEN

It was late when I woke up, well into the afternoon. I had been drifting in and out of a dream full of dead people, Danielle and Brandon and my mom. In the dream I was dead, too. I didn't mind it. It was safe, quiet. I woke to sirens singing on the nearby freeway and an image in my head, the untied lace of Brandon's shoe. I thought I could smell the air in his house, too full of him, his body turning into particles you could breathe.

I tried to sort out my thoughts: Brandon killed Danielle. The conspiracy I had imagined with Sally and the money, none of that was real. Danielle got killed because Brandon lost his temper. I still couldn't imagine it, but like Ash had said, I didn't really know the guy. I thought of him saying I didn't belong with Danielle's friends, that I deserved better. I liked how concerned he was about me—it was nice, knowing somebody cared, was paying attention. But I recalled Audrey's face as she drove away and left me on the sidewalk in front of Brandon's house. I hoped she was okay. I made coffee and texted her again, then went for a run.

I picked up a sandwich and took it home, showered, ate.

Even though I was worried about Audrey, I felt better than I had since I found out Danielle was dead. It was relief, I realized. I was glad the whole thing was resolved. And maybe I was looking forward to seeing Ash next week. I wondered when he'd call.

A knock came at the door. I opened it to Audrey, standing on the stoop. She looked terrible, like she hadn't slept, like she'd been crying since I saw her last.

"Hi," I said.

"Please," she said. "Can I come in?" Her voice shifted and cracked.

I nodded, stepped back for her to enter. She embraced me, clung to me. Her breath on my neck made me shiver.

"What happened to you?" I said.

"I'm sorry. I couldn't, I didn't, I'm sorry . . ." She was a mess.

"Come sit down," I said.

She wouldn't let go of me, she clutched my arm as I walked her to the couch.

"I'm going to get you a drink," I said. "I'll be right back."

She nodded but looked terrified. I brought the whiskey from the kitchen and poured it in glasses. I handed her one. I lit a cigarette and gave it to her.

"What'd you do? After you left?" I said.

"Finished off the coke," she said. "Drove around."

"I called you like ten times. I didn't have a ride home."

"My phone died. I was pretty fucked up. I'm sorry."

"It's okay," I said. "It's no big deal."

"The cops," she said. "What happened?"

"They said he OD'd. They asked a ton of questions."

"What'd you tell them?" she said. I'd never seen her look so anxious and vulnerable.

"Just that we went by there to check on him."

"You mentioned me?" Her voice rose in pitch. "Why did you do that?"

"You don't have to worry, Audrey. They're saying Brandon killed Danielle."

"That's bullshit."

"Audrey, listen to me. Brandon did it, then killed himself. The cops won't bother you about anything now."

"How do you know all this?"

"Ash told me."

"And you believe him," she said. "You think Brandon killed her?"

"The cops do. I didn't know him that well."

And now, I thought, I never would. I'd liked Brandon, I genuinely had. But what did I know about anything? I wasn't a cop, I wasn't even close to Danielle, not anymore. I'd never seen her and Brandon together, didn't know what they were like. There were plenty of reasons to think he was guilty.

"When did you last talk to him?" I said.

"I went over there a few days ago. A day or two after the funeral. It seems like so long ago."

"I wonder if he was already planning it then."

"What? Killing himself? He didn't say anything like that. He was crying. We talked about Danielle."

"You really don't think he could have killed her?"

"I don't trust cops," she said. "He was my friend."

Her voice fell apart at the last few words. She was shaking. She looked so frightened and confused. As much as I wanted it to all be over, I kind of agreed with Audrey. It was too hard to imagine Brandon killing Danielle. Suicide I could believe, but not murder. Not like that.

"Audrey," I said. "I'm sorry, we can talk about something else."

"Let's go somewhere," she said.

"Okay."

We took my car and traveled east along the bayou, a black emptiness that smelled like soggy garbage. We rolled down the windows and I listened to the air change pitch at each tree we passed. She loaded her pipe and handed it to me, and we smoked. Audrey seemed calmer, now that we were moving.

I followed her directions, steering the car through streets I didn't recognize until we came to a corrugated metal building with a neon Lone Star sign in the window. Inside were two pool tables, a bar, and some scattered mismatched chairs. It was muggy and smelled like stale beer and piss. Audrey engaged a squirrelly guy in whispered conversation and went with him into the men's room. I ordered Jack Daniel's, which managed to taste both watered down and too bitter. After a couple of minutes the guy walked out of the bathroom and Audrey waved me over. I took my drink in with me and she locked the door.

"It's shit, but it's not nothing," she said, unwrapping a twist of plastic.

We each had a bump. It *was* shit, dirty and speedy. A grain of it lodged in my sinus cavity. It hurt. I tried not to touch the walls in the filthy men's room, which made no sense because I undoubtedly had already snorted up whatever diseases were in there, along with the rat poison in the coke. I relaxed against the damp concrete. I was so tired of worrying about everything. It was good to surrender. I gritted my teeth. It was good.

We went to Audrey's place. She lived nearby, on the first floor of a shabby apartment complex. Her unit was bland and cheap, carpeted in beige. A thrift-store couch upholstered in pink and mauve floral tapestry stood against a windowless wall. The walls were bare, the furniture buried under clothes, magazines, half-drunk Diet Cokes.

I made an attempt to clear the table, piling crumpled receipts and dirty dishes and envelopes of Val-Pak coupons. Audrey plugged in her phone, then poured two big glasses of vodka over ice and brought them to the kitchen table. She set to work chopping the rest of the coke, smashing the crystals into dust. She held her hair and did a line before sliding the plate to me. I was glad to see her looking more like herself.

"Guess I'll have to find another gig now," she said.

I hadn't thought about the fact that she'd be out of a job. "What will you do?" I asked.

"He's not the only dude around with a video camera."

"My old job is probably hiring. You could be a barista."

"Yeah, perfect," she said. "You're hilarious." She snorted another line. "This friend of mine moved to Phoenix. She said the money's great, dancing. And it's not humid."

"Humidity's good for your complexion. I read somewhere it prevents wrinkles."

"Who cares?" she said. "It's not like we're gonna get old."

I wanted to argue with that, but then I thought of Danielle, and Brandon. My mom was thirty-nine when she died. Why would I think we'd be any different?

"We should go," Audrey said. "You and me. Why not?"

"Phoenix?" I said. It sounded like nowhere.

"Okay, how about Alaska? Brazil? Wherever."

"I don't have a passport," I said.

"Me, either. We could try California. Out west. This town is such a shithole. We could leave right now and be in El Paso in twelve hours. We're high, we won't get sleepy. Besides. What's here for me anymore?"

I looked up, moved by the desolation in her tone.

"I've always lived here," I said.

"God, I've been everywhere. I don't think I've stayed any-place a whole year since I was fifteen."

"After your mom died?"

"Yeah. And my stepdad died that same year."

"You didn't tell me that before. How awful."

"Yeah, well. I didn't care. I hated him."

"Why? What was he like?"

"He was a drunk fucking asshole. He started fucking me as soon as my mom went in the hospital."

"Shit, Audrey. How old were you?"

"Thirteen."

"Jesus."

"Yeah," she said.

She leaned over the plate and inhaled a line. She cut one for me, but I didn't want any more. I felt woozy and twitchy. Audrey took a cigarette from the pack on the table and lit it, started talking again.

"We did it every night. He was ugly . . ." She shuddered and took a sharp drag off the cigarette. "I used to get mad at my mom for marrying this ugly man. I wished he was hand-some—I thought it would be easier. I felt shitty being mad at her when she was sick, and she needed me to be strong. She always said that to me. 'Be strong for me, pumpkin.' I tried to. I tried hard. After she died . . . He drank as soon as he woke up in the mornings. He was always pissed off."

Her voice was oddly calm, didn't match what she was say-ing. I was horrified, thinking of Audrey as a child, helpless and alone. I couldn't see how she could be so fun, laugh so much, even while all this had happened to her. Maybe I'd been lucky,

with no dad around. I touched her hand across the table. She
didn't notice.

"I dressed up in her clothes for him. My mom was gorgeous,
I mean dazzling. I wore her slips and her dresses but they didn't
fit right, they were too big. He said I looked too much like her,
and he couldn't stand to see me. Before, that's why he liked me,
'cause I reminded him of her except not sick. And then, boom,
he changed his mind. He didn't like me anymore. He hated me.
It didn't matter how good I was, how hard I tried."

"Audrey, I don't understand," I said. "You wanted him to—"

"He was all I had," she said. "He wouldn't fuck me or let me
do the things he liked. Rub his neck, or get him more ice for
his drink, we didn't have to have sex. He wouldn't. He didn't
even take ice anymore, he drank from the bottle. One day he
just shoved me out and locked the door. He didn't want me. He
wanted to drink."

The bitterness in her tone scared me. She bent over the coke
and inhaled, pushed the plate to me.

"Do it," she said. "Be high with me. Please."

My heartbeat was a rapid flutter and my jaw hurt from
clenching. But how could I say no? I snorted the line she cut
for me.

"Danielle knew," she said. "Danielle knew the whole story. If
she were here I wouldn't have to talk about it."

"We don't have to," I said. "But it's good that you told
Danielle."

"Why?"

"Because she was your friend. She cared about you."

"Yeah," she said. "And now she's dead. And bloody, and . . ."

I reached across the table and hugged her. She felt stiff in
my arms.

"It's okay," I said. "You can trust me, too."

She stared at me for a second and said, "It was fucked up."

"It sounds totally fucked up. It's horrible."

"You don't even know what I'm talking about. I mean the night he died. He passed out on the couch and he wouldn't wake up. I kicked him, and all he did was groan. I took every single bottle. He drank those big handles of vodka. Half gallons. We always had extras, he was afraid of not having enough. I drank a little and poured out the rest. Splashed it on him. I had to wake him up, that's what I was trying to do. He was out cold and I just kept pouring. I soaked his clothes and the couch cushions with vodka. And the carpet around him. I spilled it everywhere. It got on the walls, the curtains, on the garbage piled up, old newspapers. I knew it was bad, but it was fun, too, like kind of satisfying."

"Shit. What'd he do?" I asked.

"He didn't wake up," she said.

"He was dead?"

"No. He died in the fire," she said.

"What fire?"

"It lit up really fast. I didn't expect that, I was only trying to wake him up."

"You set a fire?"

"I told you it was fucked up. I lit a match, and I ran and hid in our neighbor's barn and watched. It smelled terrible. I walked all night to the interstate."

"You killed him?"

"You hate me now," she said.

"No," I said. "No, of course not."

"Don't bullshit me. Tell me the truth. You hate me."

"Audrey, you were just a kid. You didn't know what you were doing."

But I watched her, wary. She rose from the table, opened a

closet door, and pulled out a duffel bag. She shoved in makeup and clothes.

"Come with me," she said.

She dropped the bag, knelt in front of me, and laid her head in my lap. I petted her hair. Her story broke my heart. I didn't know what to say. Then I realized that nothing had changed except my knowledge. Nothing had changed for Audrey. She had always lived with this—half an hour ago, five years ago. It would never leave her alone.

"Please," she said. "We could go to Hawaii."

"Hawaii sounds cool," I said.

"We could go there for Danielle. Like, to honor her."

"For Danielle? What do you mean?" I asked.

"'Cause she never got to. She was gonna move there with the money."

"What are you talking about?" I said.

"The money from the land. From her mom. She was getting a shitload. She was all excited, saying Brandon was right, with that much cash she could quit working, go off somewhere. She went there once and she loved it, she said she could live on the beach and go to massage school or some shit like that."

"But she fought with Brandon. She didn't listen to him."

Audrey shrugged. "She changed her mind. She talked to her mom and worked it out so she was getting way more money."

Sally had told me the same thing and I hadn't believed her.

"If she changed her mind, why would Brandon kill her?" I said. "It makes no sense."

"Exactly," Audrey said. "That's what I've been saying."

"How do you know all this? About the deal with Sally? How do you know about Hawaii?"

"She called me. Didn't I tell you? I went there as soon as I got her message."

"Went where?" I said. "When was this?"

"Help me pack this shit. Hey, here's your dress. I told you I'd give it back."

She tossed me the yellow sundress that she'd borrowed. I ignored it and it fell to the floor. I could hear blood beating in my head. My mind, slow and cold, tried to put it together. Danielle and Brandon fought, and Danielle went to the motel. At some point she called Audrey. Danielle changed her mind about the land, like Sally said. She talked to Sally and negotiated her new deal. Audrey went to meet her.

"You were at the motel," I said. "That's what you're telling me?"

She kept filling the bag, her back to me.

"Did you see Brandon there?" I said.

"No."

"Did you see anybody else? What time did you leave?"

"I don't know, I didn't keep track." She turned to me, stricken. "Do you think if I stayed, she'd still be alive?"

"Oh, god. You've been driving yourself crazy, haven't you?"

"I guess," she said.

"What about what's-his-name? Eddie?" I said. "The guy Danielle would meet there."

"How the fuck do you know about Eddie?"

"Ash told me."

Audrey laughed. "I forgot I told him about that. That's not even his real name. We called them all Eddie."

"What do you mean, all? How many were there?"

"I don't know, a few. It wasn't even the money. She liked it, she got off on it. Dani was so twisted."

"Well, maybe it was one of them?"

"No one was there," she said. "Just us."

"Did the cops know this? When did you leave?"

"Let's do some lines, all right? Is there any more?"

"I can't," I said. "I don't feel well. Come on, tell me what happened."

"She was saying this stuff, her big plans, and I was like, okay, cool. Hawaii, right? Let's go. But she goes, 'Audrey, I was thinking by myself. Leaving everything behind.' Like I'm what she wants to get away from."

She started to cry again, stuttering over the words. It annoyed me. I felt impatient.

"Go on," I said.

"Everybody leaves me," she said. "Everybody."

"What happened, Audrey?"

"Look, it doesn't have to be Hawaii. Let's go to California. You would like California. I've been there before. I've been to the ocean. Have you ever seen the ocean?"

"No."

"Please come with me," she said.

She hunched over the coke on the table. She was blotchy from tears, skinny and red-eyed as a drowning kitten. I could easily picture her at fifteen, hiding in a dirty barn. She didn't look pretty, or like anyone I wanted to go anywhere with. I thought of Danielle, her head beaten in, the blood.

"It was you," I said. "You killed her."

She sat in the kitchen chair, trembling, her big eyes open. She didn't say a word. She didn't say no. After a minute she took a breath and said, "Come on. We better go."

She reached for my hand and I heard a guttural animal noise coming from my own throat. I recoiled and she gripped my arm, fingernails digging into my wrist. Our eyes met. I couldn't hold her gaze.

"We can be together," she said.

"No," I said.

She was hurting me. I tried to pull my arm away from her. Her blow knocked me into the wall. I hadn't seen it coming. I shook my head, dizzy and stunned, and doubled over as she pummeled my torso with her fists. She was stronger than I thought. She hit me again and again. She kept coming at me. I used the wall for support and kicked her shin, yanked her hair, and pulled her off.

She lunged at me. I grabbed her arms and tried to hold them at her sides—if I let go she'd attack me. I shoved her down and knelt on top of her. She kicked and struggled. I didn't know how to fight. I didn't want to hurt her. I had to make her stop but I wasn't strong enough. She shoved me and I stumbled and fell. I scrambled back, to the wall behind me. The vodka bottle had rolled into the corner and I reached for it. I felt a kick to the side of my head and slumped against the wall. Audrey kicked me again and I curled into a ball over the bottle. I could hear her breathing. She leaned over, panting, her hand on the couch for support.

"You don't love me," she said.

I stared up at her. I could barely breathe.

"You always leave," she said. "Everyone leaves."

She moved towards me, knelt, and then lunged at me, her fingernails pushing at my eyes. I raised my arm, brought the bottle down on her head. The glass didn't break. The thud traveled up my arm, to my stomach, between my legs. I hit her again and the bottle broke into shards that cut my hand. She fell to her knees and collapsed sideways. I heaved, tasted vodka and bile. My body convulsed and a froth filled my head. My vision wobbled. I struggled to focus. I stayed where I was for several minutes, watching Audrey. She lay still, in a heap. I was afraid she was dead at first, but then I saw her breathing. I backed away from her, still holding the jagged broken handle of the bottle in one hand, in case she attacked me again. I ignored the blood streaming down my arm and found my phone with my other hand. I called Ash, cleaned away the drugs, and sat down on the floor. I watched Audrey's chest rise and fall, shallowly, while I waited for the sound of sirens.

CHAPTER FIFTEEN

Ash came, and some squad cars, and a team of EMTs. They put Audrey on a stretcher. Another EMT made me come with him to an ambulance parked outside. I breathed deeply and pain flexed through me. I still had spots in front of my eyes. Ash sat with me. I told him Audrey had killed Danielle. And her stepfather, a long time ago.

The EMT tended the cut on my hand, picking out shards of glass. He checked my blood pressure and my heartbeat and peered into my eyes. I didn't care if he could tell I was on drugs. Lying down was nice. Cops crammed the place, bustled around urgently. Strangely, I felt hungry. Ash got somebody to give me a candy bar, and I grew stronger with the first bite. From the back of the ambulance I watched the people come and go, talking into their phones.

They took me to the hospital and kept me overnight, for observation. My ribs weren't broken, only bruised, but the doctors were worried I had a concussion. I told them I didn't have insurance, and they let me go in the morning. I changed out of the gown they'd given me and back into my dirty clothes, smelling like vodka and rust. I took a cab to my car, still parked at Audrey's apartment complex. I got in and drove home. I slept for two days, waking periodically and swallowing the pain pills they'd given me at the hospital before drifting off again.

I woke early in the morning to the noise of the garbage truck muscling down the block. I listened to the neighborhood getting ready for work, to the rattling cart of the homeless guy who stayed in my neighbor's carport. I showered and dressed carefully, mindful of my bruised ribs.

I went out for coffee, bought the *Chronicle,* and spread the paper over the café table. I read each article carefully. Kelsey Langford was her real name. The papers talked about Danielle and Brandon, and also the fire in Nebraska, when Kelsey was fifteen. I sipped coffee and examined the articles. They'd got hold of some old photos from her high school yearbook. Sophomore year, the year of the fire. They printed a school portrait of a pale, dark-haired girl, her bangs nearly covering her eyes. Next to it was a team photo of the cheerleading squad in pyramid formation. She was second from the top. Her face was so small it looked like dots.

In the best image—a candid shot, full color—she wore her cheerleading uniform, a short skirt revealing bony teenage legs. Audrey held a soft drink can. It was fall, late afternoon. Gold light fell her face. Her lashes cast shadows. The camera had captured some element in her face of darkness, of death, of the coming winter. She looked strong and damaged, eerily adultlike.

I recognized myself in some of the articles: "Langford was apprehended after an altercation with a local woman . . ." Those people, Kelsey Langford and a local woman—they sounded like strangers. I folded the paper and left it on a bench.

Later that afternoon Ash came by. He brought flowers, a bouquet of grocery-store carnations wrapped in paper.

"How are you feeling?" he asked.

"A little better. I'll make it."

I took the flowers to the kitchen. I didn't own a vase, so I filled a tall glass with water and stuck the bouquet in it.

"Thanks for these," I said.

Ash shrugged. "I thought I'd tell you in person," he said. "She confessed to Danielle's murder. The other thing, her step-father's death, I doubt anyone will prosecute it because she was a juvenile. But she'll plead guilty to Danielle. It's really over now."

I nodded. "That's good, I guess."

Ash gave a grim smile. "There's nothing good about the way this turned out," he said. "Charlotte, I'm sorry. I put you at risk. I overlooked her. We were so focused on Brandon Young. I let you get hurt."

"I was the one hanging out with her. Like a fucking idiot."

"No," he said. "It was my responsibility. This is my job and I fucked it up. I never wanted you in the middle of it."

"I know you didn't," I said. "Listen, I'm okay. I handled it on my own. And now your case is solved."

"That's true."

"So let it go. Or, you know, say thank you or something."

"Thank you, Charlotte."

"You're welcome."

There was an awkward silence, and I wondered if he was going to bring up our dinner date. I felt tired of his guilt, his advice and protection. My side ached and I wanted to lie down, take another pill. Before he said anything, I stood up.

"I should really get some rest," I said.

"Of course. I'll go." He kissed me on the cheek. "Maybe when you're feeling better—"

"I have your number," I said.

"Right, okay. Take care, Charlotte."

"I will."

The sound of his car driving away gave me the sense that it was really, finally over. I wasn't going to call him.

I went into Common Grounds the next day to talk to Andrew about my job. I sat in the office with him for an hour and explained everything that had been going on—the fight with Audrey, her arrest.

"Things can get back to normal now," I said. "You know me, you know I've been a good employee."

He said he'd think about it and talk to the other stores, see if they needed anyone to fill in.

"That would be great," I said. "I have a car, I can go to the Heights or the Galleria. It would be even better, really."

"Okay," he said. "I'll let you know what I find out."

"Thank you," I said. I nearly hugged him.

It hurt too much to run, but I went for a long walk in the early evening once the temperature eased off. At home I sat on the steps, sweating, melting into the soft air. Sally called. She said she needed to see me.

"Can you stop by tomorrow?" she said. "It's important."

"Okay," I said, sighing. I wondered if there would ever be a time when I could say no to her.

I drove to her house the next afternoon. She answered the door wearing jeans and a faded T-shirt, her hair in a ponytail. I tried to remember if I'd ever seen her dressed that way. She looked totally different, softer, middle-aged.

"Come on in," she said.

We went to Danielle's old room. She'd kept it the same. The

old brass bed and quilt, the framed posters on the walls. Open cardboard boxes were lined up next to the closet.

"I'm cleaning," Sally said. "Getting rid of this old stuff. I thought Danielle would take it someday, but now there's no reason to keep it."

"Sally, are you sure? What if you change your mind later?"

"I won't. I'm putting the house on the market," she said. "It's too big. Too many memories."

I frowned. It was disconcerting to think Sally wasn't going to live here. This place was one of my landmarks.

"Remember this skirt?" Sally said. "She always wore it, when was that? Tenth grade?"

"Eleventh."

"It's cute. I bet it would fit you, you're so tiny. Will you take it? Can you use this stuff?"

"I guess," I said. "If you want."

"It was hers," she said. "It should go to you."

"Okay."

"There's something else, too. The real reason I wanted you to come." She picked up a large gray envelope from Danielle's old vanity and handed it to me. "Open it," she said.

Inside was a sheaf of forms from the Bank of Texas. "What is this?" I said.

"I set up a trust for you. There's half a million dollars in it. The money that would have gone to Danielle. I want you to have it."

I sat down on the bed, dropped the papers beside me. I felt a sudden vertigo.

Sally was grinning across the room at me. "Well, honey? What do you say?"

"I can't take this," I said. "It's not right."

"Sweetie, you can't *not* take it."

"It's too much," I said.

She laughed. "When it comes to cash, darlin', there's no such thing. Besides, you deserve it."

"No, I don't."

"Sure, you do. Something good for a change."

I felt claustrophobic. Half a million dollars. Jesus.

"It's not about deserving anything," I said. "Danielle didn't deserve what happened to her. Not back then, the abuse. How you let it happen. She didn't deserve to be murdered."

"Charlotte, stop it."

Her big smile was gone. I'd erased it.

"All you ever did was throw money at her. You didn't protect her. It didn't help when she was little. And then it got her killed."

"What are you talking about?"

"This is why Audrey killed her," I said. "This money is why she died. Didn't they tell you what happened?"

"Of course they told me. I'm her goddamn mother, Charlotte. I tried to help her. That woman was crazy. You can't blame me for her actions."

I stared at the thick gray envelope, felt its gravitational pull. I shuddered.

Sally was still talking, her voice softer now. "They told me how you were in the middle of it, how you figured it out. That you caught her. Charlotte, I can't imagine what it was like. It must have been horrible."

"I didn't figure anything out," I said. "Audrey told me, that's all."

"That's not what the detective said."

"He wasn't there, he doesn't know anything."

"Just take it, Charlotte." She held the envelope out to me again.

"You're only giving it to me because she's dead. It should be hers."

"You're right, it should. But that's not where we are, is it? Danielle wanted it. You should want it, too. For your future. You can do anything now. College, go to the best school you can find. Travel. You'll never have to worry, do you understand? You'll be secure."

I couldn't see it, couldn't stand the idea. Travel? Who did she think I was?

"Give it to someone else," I said. "Give it to charity. Find some organization for rape and incest survivors."

"Charlotte, stop it. You're acting like a child."

"I don't want it," I said.

"Of course you want it. It's already done, anyway. If you don't want to spend it, fine. It can sit there and accrue interest until you change your mind. You don't have a choice. It's my money and I'm giving it to you."

She picked up a stuffed animal, a unicorn with a puffy silver horn. "This was her favorite," Sally said, her voice thick with tears.

"I've never seen it before."

"Maybe you don't know everything," she said. "Did you ever consider that? I gave this to her when she was seven years old. Long before you met her. She always saved it."

Sally tossed the unicorn aside. It landed in a box of clothes.

"Charlotte, my daughter died. My *daughter*. I used to hold her in my arms. She used to run to me when I came home from work every afternoon. I've made mistakes, I know that. I've also made a lot of money. Why shouldn't I give it to you? Let this be one good thing that I have done. Please."

"You can't fix what you did to her. Money can't fix it," I said.

"Charlotte, that's not what I'm trying to do."

"Bullshit," I said. "You're using me again. I don't want to be the stand-in. You can't buy your way out of your guilt. It won't work."

"I know that," she said. "I know it's too late."

I was ready to argue, still furious, but she sounded so broken and sad I couldn't think of anything to say. She was right, I was acting like a child, ungrateful and cruel. She'd lost her daughter. What did I know about how that felt?

"Well, this isn't how I thought this would go," Sally said, her voice cold, mechanical. "Take this stuff, will you? Get it out of here." She left the room, shut the door behind her.

I stayed in there a long time, looking through the boxes. Clothes, shoes, old schoolwork, flyers for shows. Ancient history. I opened the window and smoked cigarettes like we used to back in high school. I'd slept in this room hundreds of times, woken up to the view of the oaks out the back window and Danielle in bed beside me, her scratchy legs kicking me as she dreamed. I knew the contours of the furniture in the dark, the texture of the walls. Everything was the same except for the gray envelope on Danielle's old marble-top bureau. She wasn't coming back.

I set the unicorn on the bed and started loading boxes into my car. Once they were all piled in the trunk, I went back to Danielle's room for the gray envelope. I searched the house until I found Sally, in the TV room on the third floor. She was sitting in the middle of the carpet, boxes scattered all around her. She was weeping quietly.

"Sally," I said, knocking on the open door.

She looked up.

"I don't know if I could ever pay it back," I said.

"It's a gift. I don't expect you to. I don't want anything in return."

"Yes, you do," I said. I just wanted her to know I knew.

"Okay, so I do," she said. "I want you to do something good with your life. And maybe stay in touch. It's not too much to ask, is it?"

"No, it's not too much to ask."

"So you'll take it?"

I nodded.

"Good," she said.

She stood and came to me, put her arms around me. I hugged her back. Her child was dead. She didn't have to do this for me. She didn't have to think about me at all, but she was. Maybe that was a kind of love.

"Thank you," I whispered.

"You're welcome."

She walked me to the front door and kissed me on the cheek.

Behind the wheel, I eased the car out of River Oaks. It was getting dark. The outside air vibrated around me. Cicadas whined in the trees, and a slow wet breeze signaled summer beginning. The city felt gentle and open. I cruised west on Memorial, taking the curves through the golf course. The reflective stripes of runners' shoes flashed along the trail. At the Loop I entered the on-ramp. I remembered driving this way with Audrey, that night after the funeral. It seemed impossibly long ago, and innocent. We were on our way to buy coke; we were sad and we wanted to feel better.

I veered onto the Northwest Freeway. I passed the tollway and kept driving, floating through the endless neighborhoods of identical houses, the culs-de-sac lined with progressively younger trees. At Fry Road the land emptied into darkness, no shape discernible beyond the white-lit lanes of the freeway. I parked along the shoulder and sat on the trunk of the car with a cigarette, studying the glow to the east that was my city. Nothing but gray light at the bottom of the sky. A truck's wake washed over me, the force of air so strong I could have let it knock me down.

I knew Sally was right—I could do something good with the money. College or whatever. I could apply to schools all over the country. Decide where I wanted to live. I had no idea how to spend that kind of money, or what to want. But I had plenty of time to figure it out.

On my way back to town I stopped by a Goodwill and piled Danielle's boxes in front of the donations door. Afterwards my car felt lighter, zipped easily down the freeway. I went to the Fiesta in my neighborhood. I put apples in my basket, pasta, cereal and yogurt, cheese and bread. At home I put the groceries away and made a sandwich. It seemed like years since I'd done such a simple, normal thing.

ACKNOWLEDGMENTS

Enormous gratitude to the Ucross Foundation and the Mississippi Arts Council for their generous support while I was working on this book. Thank you to my friends and readers: Tom Franklin, Alexander Chee, Mary Miller, Richard Lange, Megan Abbott, Ace Atkins, Deborah Barker, Jennifer Adrian, Beth Troncoso, Kelly Wilson, and Lindsay Schnetzer.

I owe a debt to Henry Dunow for believing in this project and coaxing it into shape. Thanks to my agent, Duvall Osteen, and my editors, Zachary Wagman and Angus Cargill.

Most of all, thank you to Chris Offutt, for everything, everything.